Praise for

THE ARCHIVE OF ALTERNATE ENDINGS

"Captivating ... Drager's plot is ambitious and emotionally resonant, making for a clever, beguiling novel."

—*Publishers Weekly* starred review

"A philosophical novel ... beautiful in its conception."

—*Kirkus Reviews*

"Drager's intoxicating novel presents itself like the box in Schrödinger's famous cat experiment. Until you open the box, the cat is both alive and dead. Drager seems to be saying that 'We are part of a system, for better and for worse.' A system that includes labyrinths and dark forests as well as siblings, light, and houses made of ginger bread. ... What a pleasure it is to enter the safe harbor of Drager's novel."

—*The New York Journal of Books*

"A leaner, tighter, more emotionally impactful take on connectedness and purpose and the immensity of existence than David Mitchell created with *Cloud Atlas*—done in a quarter of the pages, with a more sincere, human touch. There isn't a grand conspiracy or plot here. This is a book about life. The result is a bold novel that challenges the idea of storytelling, time, identity, love, family, and history. Someone once told me that the best books haven't been written yet. This one has."

—*Barrelhouse*

"Drager has developed somewhat of a cult following her previous books ... and for good reason—her writing is ling love, queerness, time and space, an and poetic read."

—*Brooklyn*

"There is something both nihilistic and deeply hopeful in Drager's looping novel. Nihilistic, because in so many ways it indicates that as parts of a continuum of human storytelling, life, love, and hate, none of us matter; but hopeful because that continuum means our stories are related, our narratives interlocking, and so while we may be insignificant, we are also never alone."

—*NPR*

"Drager has a unique ability to breathe life into some of history's most unique and unassuming characters, from world-famous scientists and Renaissance thinkers, to the fictional personalities of Hansel & Gretel... For a story that feels hopelessly predestined at times, there is an incredible amount of cerebral introspection, suspense, and philosophy here to delight even the most cynical reader. As *The Archive of Alternate Endings* implies, we are all connected through our stories, and folklore is the carefully curated history of the world laid bare."

—*Michigan Quarterly Review*

"[A] taut, deeply philosophical retelling ... This is a profoundly resonating book that will feel both dense and light."

—Historical Novel Society

"Although relatively slim, Drager's novel is a vast and convoluted treasure trove. She does a fine job of illuminating the darker concepts and human relationships with her rich, confident, and sometimes startling writing. Reading *The Archive of Alternate Endings* is an enriching literary experience the reader will remember hauntingly ever after."

—Philly.com

THE AVIAN HOURGLASS

A NOVEL

LINDSEY DRAGER

DZANC
BOOKS

DZANC
BOOKS

5220 Dexter Ann Arbor Rd.
Ann Arbor, MI 48103
www.dzancbooks.org

Library of Congress Cataloging-in-Publication Data Available Upon Request

ISBN: 9781950539970
First US edition: August 2024
Interior design by Michelle Dotter
Cover design by Steven Seighman

Printed in the United States of America

10   9   8   7   6   5   4   3   2   1

THE AVIAN HOURGLASS

180

Luce once explained that her fathers taught her to compose a globe like this: first, you craft two half spheres, and then you cut these thin strips of map to fit over it. You can't just make an orb and then wrap it in a single atlas—the shapes will disagree. What you have to do is form these sort of crescent-moon-shaped bands of map—thick at the middle, then tapered so they thin at the top and bottom—and glue them on, one at a time, until the bottom of the sphere is covered. Then you do the top half, and only finally fit them together to make the world whole.

We were sitting in the bed of her truck. Aunt Luce took a long drag on her cigarette, ashed over the side, ran her hand over her crew cut as she told me about how her fathers—my grandfathers— were deeply, madly in love, and globemaking is what brought them together, like the southern and northern hemispheres. Of course, I already knew that. Luce caught me rolling my eyes. She asked if I was listening to her—had I heard her, the way she meant me to?

"What I am saying is this," she said, looking up into the sky. "You don't just apply the map to the territory. You have to build the world, construct the terrain of the earth, one thin ribbon at a time."

179

Six months after the birds disappear, I discover Saturn. Saturn is a small cement block I come upon on a long walk down a gravel road that used to lead out of town. Now the road leads nowhere, stops at a dead end in a field. Before I find Saturn, I am walking and breathing and reflecting on the way it seems The Crisis is coming to a tipping point, and things could either get much better or things could get much worse, and whichever way it goes, it will go that way soon. I have faced the dead end of this road many nights, but on this night, I feel something growing from something else, one event causing another. I am thinking of the eclipse that we just witnessed, our town set firmly in the path of totality.

I have failed the test again. The test being the first step in pursuing the life I want, which is the life of a radio astronomer. I have failed the test four times, and that means I have one last and final chance—one single opportunity—to pass the test and get on with my dream.

It is all of this—the eclipse, The Crisis, my failures—that whisper in my ear to keep going when I reach the end of the road. The road leads nowhere, but in that moment, for the first time ever, I step beyond its end.

Since the eclipse, the blood inside me aches. There's a dread I can't shake. Our town saw the entire sun covered by the moon, and the world went dark for a second and then when the world reappeared, the dread entered me, traveled straight through my veins to my heart where it has been lodged firmly ever since.

The degree of the dread is substantial.

I am lost as to when it will leave.

I walk five, twelve steps into the field, into the phantom, spectral road-that-once-was. I imagine that I am a baby bird, and while I have been expelled from my mother, it's up to me to choose the time to break out of my shell. It is then I see something on the ground. I crouch down and pull the tall grass away and it is a cement block, once painted bright blue but now faded and aged from time and weather. At first I think it is a gravestone, but I can see the impression of Saturn, the ringed planet, and I can see the word *Saturn* set in the cement. It is a marker, sure as rain, but not for someone gone. I think the font is really beautiful, and because I have just given life to the dead end of the road, I go back to a time in the long past, possibly before I was born, when the road led somewhere, when this block was new and fresh and someone chose this spot—this very precise location—to place Saturn. Perhaps it was one person or more than that. Perhaps it was many people. Saturn, I say aloud, and finger the rings around the planet and pull out my pocketknife and cut away small pieces of Earth that have grown over Saturn's edges.

It occurs to me that I've never discovered anything. I'm not a discoverer. I'm a bus driver who is about to lose her job to automation. I'm the legal guardian of a set of triplets. I'm the one who occupies the north side of the duplex I share with Uri. I am not many things, but in the middle of The Crisis, many things that once weren't now are.

It is dusk and I have found Saturn, and on my way home I recite some of the lines of Uri's play.

178

Luce tells me that the etymology of the word *crisis* comes from the Late Middle English for turning or decisive point and the Greek for decision, often in relation to disease.

I will pass the test this time, I tell myself. I will pass the test and I will do the thing that I was born to do, which is be a radio astronomer. I put toe to heel as I walk home from Saturn and begin studying yet again. In my mind, I review Einstein's field equations. Maxwell–Heaviside equations. Thomson scattering. Fusion power. Guiding centers. The first fifty decimal digits of pi.

177

When I arrive home, I knock on Uri's side of the duplex. The door opens and the triplets hug my legs and the five of us—the triplets and Uri and I—eat our dinner on the porch because the evening is beautiful. As he is cutting up the broccoli for the triplets and negotiating how many bites they still need to take, I decide to tell him I've failed the test a fourth time. He looks at me with a face that says he's sorry, but I tell him the previous tests were just practice. It's the next one that I'll pass.

The triplets want to visit one of the giant nests before bed, and because the American robin's is closest to our duplex, we go there. No one knows who is putting the nests up but everyone knows why. Since the birds disappeared, we find ourselves mourning in large and small ways.

At the nest, Uri lifts each triplet inside and I touch the outside and he tells me that his problem is the end. Last year, when there were still birds, Uri was asked by the local arts council to write a play about the paradox of The Crisis. He was thrilled and elated, then immediately uneasy and overwhelmed. It took me a while to learn this is simply how artists behave. Most of the play is written, has been for a long while, except the end. It's the end he can't decide on. He says that a play is a living thing, and to end a living thing is a great responsibility.

When he says this, I nod, but inside me I hold firm to the knowledge that I do not understand.

The triplets are humming as they lie in the nest. They wiggle their bodies so all three of them can lie down and they look to me like a human tessellation. Their humming is jarring—the triplets are not in tune—and therefore their song is a bit eerie. But all at once their discord locks into order and I realize someone must have taught them how to sing a round.

We take the long way home right through the center of town. When we pass the sundial, we all do a loop around it for good luck. This is customary, one of our tiny town's oldest traditions. But the triplets are acting strange this evening—in truth, their mood has been ever stranger since the eclipse—and they keep making circles around the sundial, until finally Uri grabs two and I grab the last one and we start toward home. I run definitions in my head: the difference between a quark and a lepton. The SI unit of viscosity.

When they are in bed, the triplets beg me to read their favorite retelling of Girl in Glass Vessel. But since the birds disappeared, Uri and I have mutually decided they do not need to hear this or any version of Girl in Glass Vessel, a story about a woman who lives in a world without birds. That story was once fable and now—because of The Crisis—it is fact, and Uri and I don't know yet how to navigate a conversation about a world in which the line between what is real and what is artificial doesn't exist anymore.

Instead, I read them their favorite version of Chicken Little, put on my old cassette tape of the sounds of outer space, shut their door, and listen to them murmur to each other as they fall asleep. In my bedroom, I glance at my piles of astronomy and physics books, my notepads and charts, my dry erase board. I need to study, but instead I decide to look out the window with my third-hand telescope to try to see if I can make out even a single star. Of course, the light and air pollution is too great so all I see is the delicate curving patterns of the smog.

Uri says that the most magical element of theater is the way that the audience is convinced to suspend their disbelief. It's something sublime that theater can do this, he says, that theater can will the spectators into permitting the stage to become this portal of access to the private worlds of the characters before them.

That is what I'm thinking when I look into the sky without stars. The Crisis is here, and very soon I will no longer drive the bus because the bus will drive itself. I have one more chance—one last chance to pass this test. I have one more shot to begin the journey toward being the person I am not yet, but will eventually become.

There are no more visible stars. I point my telescope toward the area of the sky where Polaris would be this time of year, if we could see it.

Saturn lives just beyond the road that leads nowhere, I think, adjusting the scope, and I guess in that regard it doesn't lead nowhere anymore.

176

There's a photograph of my grandfathers on my refrigerator, given to me by Luce. PaPa is behind Grandad, his arms swung around Grandad's neck, and Grandad's hands are crossed in front of him so that the photo centers on their four hands and twenty threaded fingers. PaPa's face is hidden in Grandad's hair, but you can tell by his eyes that he's smiling. Grandad is mid-laugh, and he's looking up at the clouds.

The photograph might be my favorite ever taken. It might be the gift offered to me that I love best. I spend time looking at it every morning, every time I reach inside the fridge to get whatever it is the triplets need. I only remove it when I slip it into the pocket of my overalls each time I leave the house to take the test.

But it's only today, after test four, as I am placing it back on the refrigerator that I see in the background, in the distance, far away, at the top of the picture and to the left of Grandad's head there is a bird, midflight, wings stretched out, gliding in the sky.

175

The massive nests began to sprout around our town a week or so after the eclipse. So far there are four, each about the size of a garden shack. When the first nest surfaced we found it strange, then beautiful. But after a few days of regular visits, an older one among us—

Sulien, who used to birdwatch back when there were birds—took notice of the construction.

"It's uncanny. Look here. It perfectly mimics a real yellow warbler nest. The hard, larger sticks and branches on the outside for sturdiness when situated in the tree. Then the weave of soft grasses toward the center. The structure tall and deep. Also, the floor: hair and fur and plant fuzz. To ensure the eggs won't break. To confirm the chicks stay warm."

"It's a mystery!" Uri exclaimed.

"It's extraordinary," I replied.

"It's a memorial to a lost species," Sulien said, "and I think we should get in."

The three of us climbed into the deep divot in the middle and looked up at the sky.

"Is this what it was like to be a bird?" Uri asked.

"Don't anthropomorphize," Sulien told us. "No one knew what it meant to be a bird, and no one will ever know now."

174

The triplets are down for a nap when I get online to schedule my fifth test. When I log into the portal, there is an all-caps, red box warning reminding me, essentially, that it's this time or never. I cannot fail again. In my last four attempts I have grown more familiar with the test, the nature of the questions, the structure and pacing and form. Sometimes, in life, it takes a second try, a third. Sometimes it takes a fifth. I register for my seat at the testing site and I circle the date in black marker on the calendar next to my bed.

I have three months to conduct the work that must be done to make the life I need to lead. Three months, I think, and I run the prime numbers through my head.

173

I had not intended to drive the bus for the last seven years, but I had not intended to be the legal guardian of the triplets, either. My déjà vu—which is severe and comes in waves that require I sit down and breathe very slowly—has gotten much worse since the eclipse. In fact, I have started to reframe the notions of intention and causation altogether. Luce tells me the word *effect* comes from the Old French and Latin for completion, result, accomplishment, and ending. *Intent*, she says, comes from *intend*, which in Old French means to stretch or extend. The problem is this: the idea of having intention—the idea of having control over effects by altering their causes—seems silly when my déjà vu confirms for me that every move I make was meant to be.

This is how I know I'll pass the test. I wish I knew if I were getting better, but my world is a world of binaries. Pass or fail. On or off. YES or NO.

I am thinking about this as I make my rounds on Route 0 today, the route I've been assigned for the last seven years. After my shift is over, I pull the bus into the depot and remember that my time at the helm is growing slim. While I don't know the exact date yet, I've been told the end is coming and to prepare.

On the long walk home, as I am reviewing the difference between centripetal acceleration and centrifugal force, I decide to visit the community center. There are a series of folding chairs facing the wall we dedicated to the memory of birds, and we encourage community members to come here to reflect. The NO people and their families come Tuesdays, Thursdays, and Sundays, and the YES people visit on Mondays, Wednesdays, and Fridays. Saturdays are for The Demonstration, so no one comes at all, which is why I do my reflecting then.

The Bird Wing is covered in photographs and drawings and anecdotes. I search to try to find the image of birds the triplets drew. I will admit it is a bit disturbing—a series of black Vs that somehow have dimension, so that they are smaller in the top and sides of the picture and grow bigger toward the middle and bottom until it looks like they are coming out of the wall and into the viewer's face. And the way they are all made with scratches of black crayon, always taking that V shape. It's a bit unsettling, but children as a rule are unsettling, so I find a way to be both unsettled and also proud.

I have contributed my own tales to the wall. Of the time I saw a piping plover fake a wing injury to capture the attention of some human children threatening her young. Of the time I saw a flock of crows gather in silence with bowed heads as they looked over the corpse of one of their own. Of my father returning to me as a cardinal, then following and visiting me for years, and how, now that the birds are gone, it feels like he's died all over again.

It seems I am alone when I hear someone clear their throat, and when I look over, there, sitting in another folding chair, is Sulien.

We sit for a while in silence, which is my favorite state to be in with Sulien. Every other person in this world makes me feel uncomfortable with silence, except for him. I do not yet know why.

"I failed the test again," I tell him. "So now I've only got this one last try. It'll happen, I know. But I wish it weren't taking so long."

He nods to me and we stay silent for a while. I am watching the wall of bird ephemera and defining Bernoulli's principle, then Pascal's principle, then the parallel axis theorem when suddenly Sulien speaks.

"Hummingbirds," he says, still staring at the wall. I try to make out what he's looking at, perhaps a photograph or a short poem, a chart comparing the size of various eggs.

"Hummingbirds?" I ask.

"I overheard you ask Luce last week if any bird could fly backward. The answer is hummingbirds," Sulien says again. "They were the only ones."

172

In the tower, at the window's ledge. Day.

> *Curtain up on ICARUS, who faces the audience, which is the window. His father is offstage, but can be heard tinkering. ICARUS should be nervous throughout the play, uncomfortable in his own skin. Trying to discern who he is and who he isn't.*
>
> *ICARUS is hugging himself when the curtains open. A few beats pass as he holds himself in this uncomfortable manner. Offstage, his father's work can be heard. Then, after some time, ICARUS spreads wide his arms to the audience and begins to speak.*

171

After I leave Sulien, I decide to swing by Saturn. It feels strange to walk beyond the end of the road, but now that I know there is something celestial buried in the field, I trick myself into believing the laws of the world have been revised, like my grandfathers' globes, and every end is really a beginning.

When I get home, I peek in on the triplets. The old boombox Luce fixed up for me is playing a cassette tape of the sounds of space. Uri thinks I'm strange for not streaming the audio from the internet, but I have always firmly believed in the intimate nature of analog. It's important to me to teach the triplets how to listen in both new and old ways, and the sounds of space from the cassette tape help them fall asleep.

On the days Aunt Luce watches the triplets, she waits for me in the bed of her truck which is parked on the street in front of our duplex so we can sneak a cigarette. She was my father's twin, and sometimes when I look at her as she talks, I can trick myself into believing I'm speaking with a version of him.

Luce is wearing her standard outfit—gray jumpsuit that is too large for her frame, rolled sleeves and pants to make it fit better. Embroidered patch on the left that says *Luce*; embroidered patch on the right that has the emblem of The Server Farm. Handkerchief poking out of her left back pocket. Steel-toed boots.

I tell her that I've failed the test, again, but her response tells me she already knew. My plan, I tell her, is to double my study hours, widen the scope of fields to fold in some quantum mechanics and astrobiology—my weak areas—and nail it this last time. She gives me a look that I can only interpret as neutral. Then she looks up at the sky and tells it—or rather, tells me—that she believes in me. She uses precisely those words, "I believe in you," and the sound of them inside my mind feels like a hand squeeze. I am believed in, I think. Aunt Luce believes.

Then she tells me there is a spot opening up in management at The Farm and she's looking to advance.

The Server Farm is relatively new. The building used to house The Factory, but when it shut down, the building was bought by a tech company, remodeled, and turned into The Farm.

I never knew what The Factory made, nor if it made anything whole at all—perhaps it just made parts that were assembled somewhere else. I have never asked Luce, and Luce has never told me. What I know is this: it is The Factory that has kept this small town running, The Factory that has kept our town alive. Now that The Factory is The Farm, it's hard to tell what will happen.

"This position, it's harder work," she says. "More responsibility. But the pay," she says.

"You up for the challenge?" I ask her.

"Feels wrong not to try. What about you? Any timeline on the route?"

"Nothing yet." We are quiet for a while, the smoke from our cigarettes coiling upward to join the starless sky. "The test," I say. "It's in three months. Just enough time," I tell her, and she looks at her shoes.

Luce blows smoke from her nostrils. "The triplets were fine to-night. A bit wound up. They keep talking about black holes. Any idea where they're getting that from?"

"None. They've been acting weird since the eclipse."

She waits a bit and then, running her hand along her head, she says, "*Eclipse*. Middle English, Old French. Derived from the Latin and Greek *ekleipsis* meaning 'to leave.'"

170

That evening in bed, as I'm trying to get to sleep, I find myself struggling with my déjà vu. It comes on often and at moments when I already feel unstable, which makes me even less in command of the thoughts in my head and the dread in my veins.

I know that déjà vu is just a trick of the brain, that the events you are living are not actually repeated, that it is simply your mind remembering the trace of a trace of an experience, and this new experience happening now is transposing itself over that memory to make it feel like you've done this before.

But sometimes, when I'm driving the bus and I fall into one of my afternoon lulls where there's no traffic, and I get to thinking I'm the only one on the road, the only one in this town, the only one driving here or anywhere at all—sometimes I let myself think that my déjà vu is an echo of something still to come, an experience offered to me in a dream so long ago that I could not have imagined the person I was watching was a future version of me.

And now—now that my life has met and matched up with that future I was fed in my dreams as a child—now I know that everything's unfolding in just the right way, that I was supposed to do the things I've done and encounter this moment in precisely and exactly this manner.

It isn't real—it's my imagination—but this is what I think Uri means when he says that in order to let art move you, you can't just believe. You have to be aware that you're pretending. You have to know it's not real but choose to think it is anyway.

169

Another nest surfaces a week later, when another seven days of studying have been crossed off my calendar. Today I'm on electromagnetism and tomorrow is fluid mechanics.

The new nest is attached to the side of the elementary school. I see it from the windows of the bus, and when my shift is over and I get home, I ask Uri to feed the triplets so I can investigate. Works for him, he says, since he needs to know their thoughts on the new ending he's drafted for the play.

When I arrive at the nest, Sulien is already there inspecting the work.

"Did you know time operated more slowly for birds? Really all animals with high metabolism and small bodies." I look up because it has suddenly started to drizzle. "For them, a single drop of rain falling was sluggish. Imagine."

Sulien opens his umbrella, gestures for me to join him underneath.

"See here?" He lets his hand run along the side of the nest. It's made of something that looks like stucco. "It's a perfect replica of a barn swallow nest. Just scaled up and reinforced at the bottom. Probably since humans are more dense than birds. I think the artist wants them to be used."

"Are we calling the maker an artist?" I ask him, and he shrugs. I touch the outside of the nest, feel the texture of the hardened mud mixed with thick grasses and hay.

"What would you say the visual field for a human is?" he asks.

I lean down to tie my shoe, and he squats, keeping the umbrella over me. "Maybe 90 degrees?"

"It's 120, including peripheral vision. But pigeons. Pigeons had a visual field of 300 degrees. Imagine how you would be changed by seeing that much," he says. He stays squatting, so I do, too. "Makes you consider how, based on your position in the world, your understanding of it differs." He looks up at the nest towering above us. "There is no single reality, you know? Just a warping, weaving cluster of the real."

Slowly we rise together and stand, listening to the rain on the umbrella, admiring the human-sized nest. Then very suddenly he hands me the umbrella and gets inside. "It was the bones," he says, patting the space next to him, "that made birds less dense than humans." I give him back the umbrella and get in, too, and we can see across the way that the sun is setting. But I understand then what he means—the sun isn't doing anything. It's the earth that moves.

"The bones of birds were empty," Sulien says. We sit there together, watching the night sky emerge starless but illuminated, almost radioactive, like a glowing wound.

168

ICARUS: *[Standing on the window ledge.]* The flight paths of the past, though spectral, frame the future.

167

ONE OF THE TRIPLETS: What were birds?
HER: Birds are— Were. Birds were small beasts. With wings and feathers. Who can— Could. Who flew. *[She sighs.]* Small beasts who— Who used to— Shit.

ANOTHER OF THE TRIPLETS: Small beasts who used to shit?

HER: No. Language! Winged beasts. Who had feathers. And laid eggs. [*Beat.*] They were an animal.

THE THIRD OF THE TRIPLETS: Uri, what were birds?

URI: What's that? [*To her.*] Laundry's done and ironed. I used that new detergent. It's fantastic! Smells like my youth. And here's dinner: three-cheese broccoli macaroni bake.

HER: [*She sighs.*] Never, ever leave us.

URI: Not a chance.

ONE OF THE TRIPLETS: Uri! What were birds?

URI: What's that? Oh, birds. Birds were creatures who instilled in us a desire to make our bodies fly while reminding us that we never would.

166

The night the weaver bird nest goes up, wrapped around the swing set at the park, Uri decides to perform the entire play for me—right up until Act 3, Scene 4, which he characterizes as The Beginning of the As-Yet-Undecided End. After the triplets are down, I squeeze in an hour of studying thermodynamics, then arrange myself on a blanket spread over the tiny patch of grass that is our front yard. Uri stands on our shared front porch to simulate the stage. He calls it a dry run, and when I raise my beer and give him a puzzled look, he waves me off, says it's shop talk and to listen closely, make mental notes about what isn't working. He turns his back to me. The wings he wears are terribly uneven on his shoulders, but I don't say anything. Then, very slowly, he turns to face me—Uri's version of curtains up—and the play begins.

Uri is the brother of the woman for whom my body was a surrogate. I was five weeks away from giving birth to their triplets when the parents died in a car accident. Before they'd left that last time, they'd each hugged me very tightly and kissed me on the forehead. I took one of each of their hands and placed it on my stomach, and the three of us on the outside touched the skin wall between the three of them on the inside. Uri broke the news to me in a phone call two days later, said he was still in shock. I told him I was sorry about his sister, and he wept. Then he collected himself and asked me what I planned to do.

That night I got out my telescope and tried like hell to see the stars. I saw nothing.

When I called Uri back the next morning and told him I was going to raise them, he asked if I was sure. I sighed very loudly and said yes. We were quiet for a minute, and then he told me that his sister had changed their wills so I had some money coming. "Also," he said, "I'd like to help." At first I thought he meant visiting on weekends, providing the cake for birthdays, offering his only living relatives his last name. But what he meant was taking the early retirement buyout from the insurance company where he worked so he could afford a duplex, placing me on one side and himself on the other. He'd be a second parent, he said, and pursue his real passion which, it turned out, was playwriting.

He helped me navigate the legal system to get custody, held my hand through the labor, gave me breaks to sleep for the ten months after birth, and for the last four years he has cooked every one of my evening meals—every one—delivering them to my side of the duplex at 6 p.m. sharp. He is twenty-seven years older than me and he's never been in love and he wears his hair in a braid and he irons the triplets' clothing as a form of relaxation. He is a wicked chess player, a fantastic masseuse, a force to reckon with in karaoke. He is my best friend.

We are in the middle of Act 3, Scene 3, and Uri is reciting the soliloquy that could be considered the climax. His play is a one-man, Theater of the Absurd retelling of the Icarus myth. He is trying to challenge assumptions about the self by having the actor occupy the position of both Icarus and Daedalus, to embody in one form both father and son. It is about the paradox of The Crisis, after all, he tells me—that generational conundrum.

Uri shrugs his shoulders to adjust his wings, which he has fashioned himself from old metal hangers and a pair of nylons. They look ridiculous but they do the work of getting him into character. He launches into the lines that are my favorite: Daedalus warning his son that he needs to find the right height—that he can't fly too close to the sun or the wax will melt from the heat, but can't fly too close to the sea or the wax will dissolve from the salt.

Uri has memorized the play, and while I know many lines, having listened to Uri perform excerpts in this manner over the years, I've never seen the whole thing put together. I feel the end of Act 3 approaching, since this is the only scene where he directly addresses the audience and I always get chills. Then Uri goes silent, and instead of turning around to signify the curtains have closed, he slumps down to sit on the porch, his legs swinging over the edge.

"That's as far as I've got. That's where The End begins." I hand him his beer and he takes a swig, adjusts his wings again, and pulls the pen from behind his ear in preparation for my feedback.

"I would add a pause after 'the loose feathers of ancient transgressions' at the end of Act 1, turn your face to the left—not the right—during the confession at the beginning of Act 3, and shift into a rough whisper at the place where you've left off: the beginning of The End. Other than that, it sounds great."

He nods and makes the notes on the inside of his palm. Then he reaches out his beer neck and I lean in and click mine to his and the sound is superb.

165

Luce is throwing rocks at my window, trying to get me to come down. I drag myself away from my desk, wave my astronomy book at her, then hold up my finger to note I'm on my way.

Luce hands me the cigarette she's been smoking and tells me I'm working too hard. I tell her that is the point. The test, I tell her, is the thing anchoring me to the way forward. But she says that I am letting the world go by. A seventh nest has gone up. This one belongs to the bald eagle. Then she says that the word *nest* comes from the Indo-European word for nether, meaning down, below, or sit. I lie next to her in the bed of her truck and breathe in deeply, listening to the sounds of space from the triplets' room through the baby monitor. I take a drag here and there and she asks me what I was studying and I tell her about the axis of evil—that relationship between the cosmic microwave background and the plane on which the solar system rests.

She grunts a laugh and shakes her head and then Luce is quiet for a moment before she says that there are several words that do not have a clear etymology. It's too difficult to track their meaning through the ages, she says, primarily because sound leaves no record, or it didn't then. As words morph into other words when they are spoken, their meaning morphs, too, and in some cases, there is no clear way to map the path back to their origin.

Words that have this problem are left in limbo. While we have some idea of how they might have evolved, their real source is only a guess.

"What are some words like that? Words without a known history?" I ask her, handing her a new cigarette.

Luce runs her hand over her shaved head. "*Girl*," she says.

I turn my face to look at her, but her eyes are closed.

"*Bad*," she says. And then, a minute later, "*Curse*."

And then, after a really long silence, Luce says: "*Bird*."

I let myself think briefly then of the day after I pass the test, when the whole of my family will hug me, hold me, congratulate me on the work I have done to pursue the life of a radio astronomer. I will tell them that this work is the work of protection, shielding them and the rest of our town, our planet, from celestial dangers. I imagine I pass the test and this becomes my ticket to a life full of recording frequencies from space, then mapping the location of celestial objects based on sonic vibrations. Not just the stars, but other phenomena: exoplanets, dark matter, as well as approaching asteroids and other interstellar threats. The test will be passed, I think then, and I close my eyes, smelling the cigarette smoke. Because if the test is not passed, then everything—my whole world—becomes slippery and fragile.

If I don't pass this test—which I will, I can feel it in the blood in the veins of my body—then the entirety of my future moves from the realm of possibility and chance, opportunity and options, to something else, something wrong, something fuzzy and undefined that is too far away for me to see.

164

ICARUS: *[Seated, his father adhering the wax to his back.]* Somewhere in the cosmos, Earth's twin reveals our mirror-lives.

163

On the day of the eclipse, Uri told me he was certain this event would inspire him to end the play.

"In the story of Icarus, the antagonist is the sun," Uri had said, and then gestured upward.

"Isn't the antagonist the father?" I responded, but he waved my thought away.

It was not a coincidence that our town was directly in the path of totality, he told me. There was meaning in the fact that he was here, with me, in this town. He was certain his answers were coming, he said as we finished tying all six shoes on the triplets' feet.

The town was convinced no one would be able to see anything. Our skies had been smog-filled for nearly a decade, and that morning was no exception. By the afternoon, the clouds were completely covering the sky. Of course, no one was all that distraught, since they hadn't had much hope in the first place.

But then, an hour before it was supposed to happen, the sky emerged. All the smog and dirty clouds dissolved. It hadn't been that clear for nearly eleven years. The last time it had been that clear, I'd seen stars, though I didn't pay attention at the time since I didn't know I would so seldom see them after.

This was the day before I would fail the test for the third time.

When the clouds parted that way—when the sky grew suddenly clear and transparent an hour before the eclipse—Uri said it was the house curtains opening. The show was about to begin.

162

At The Demonstration—which has been going on for four decades now and so different generations call it other things, like The Rally or The March—there are always two sides. On one, many young adult people argue YES. On the other, a similar number of young adult people argue NO.

My heart lies in neither side but it is part of the local culture to participate so in the interest of fairness I demonstrate for both. When on the YES side, there is optimism and hope which the NO side says is false and misleading. When on the NO side, there is cynicism and fact-facing which the YES side says is not productive in inaugurating change.

The truth is I believe we are all really hurting because of The Crisis, especially since the last bird disappeared. I believe when we

reached the end of birds—birds, whose genetic code outlived dino-
saurs—people realized we were at the precipice of a whole new para-
digm of being.

I try to stay apolitical, which should be easy, but I only sort of
succeed by playing for both sides. That I have a choice at all means I
have an advantage, and I don't forget that.

But sometimes, when I'm on one side and I see someone on the
other side whose face I was applying sunscreen to the day before,
whose voice I have matched in chant and whose hand I have held in
solidarity, I have a thought that perhaps we have mistakenly identified as sides what are in fact two responses to the same threat, and
if only we really sat down and talked about it, maybe cried about it,
perhaps made art about it, we would come to realize this fact.

When I think about what it will take to bring us together, I believe it would have to be a very beautiful and wordless song, one that
requires a new scale of sound that hasn't been discovered yet. Then I
remember that birds taught early humans to sing, and I grow overwhelmed by the notion of change and want everything—even The
Demonstration—to stay strictly, completely, exactly as it is.

161

ONE OF THE TRIPLETS: What were stars?

HER: No, no, what *are* stars. Stars still exist, we just can't see them.
To us, if you could see them, they would look like tiny specks of
light, but in truth they are suns, the centers of entirely other planetary systems that we can only vaguely imagine.

ANOTHER OF THE TRIPLETS: Stars are suns?

HER: And the sun is a star. Everything is about how you choose to look.

THE THIRD OF THE TRIPLETS: You look tired.

HER: Thank you for acknowledging that.

160

"Any news about your route?" Luce asks. She has just finished telling me she's applied for that opening in management at The Farm, is waiting to hear back. It was Luce's turn to watch the triplets, and they are now down for the night. I can hear Uri working on the play inside his side of the duplex, performing the lines. From what I can hear, Icarus is on the ledge of the tower window, about to take flight.

"Not yet," I tell her. She lights my cigarette.

"I'm not going to tell you what to think," she says, "but something about it feels wrong." I breathe in the nicotine and wave her off but she goes on. "Used to be all you worried about was the The Factory. Then the receptionists lost work, the data entry folk, then everyone in delivery services. Now a self-driving bus?" she says, using her thumb to press on a rust spot in the truck's bed. "Next it'll be robot nannies."

"I don't know," I say. "It turns out 95% of bus accidents happen because of human mistakes."

Luce rolls her shoulders and looks up at the blank, wide sky. "I'll tell you this much. This much I know. 100% of accidents happen because of human mistakes. I've never heard of an accident in nature." She looks at me then and ashes over the side of the truck but doesn't break her stare. "A year or two into this self-driving world—you just wait. I get it when it comes to the cities, but out here, in our no-name town? I mean, hell," she says, more softly. "Keep going this direction, soon the world won't need people."

"Exactly," I say.

I get the feeling she thinks I'm agreeing, but I mean it in a different way.

Driving the bus was supposed to be temporary. The plan was to work full time for a few years after high school to save up for tuition, then enroll at the community college to knock out the gen eds. But then I moved out of Aunt Luce's place and had to make rent. At first I worked as a receptionist at the waste management center, until they realized I was expendable—all they needed was a bell and an answering machine. When I lost that job, what I had was a GED, good references, and no driving record. The surrogate gig with Uri's sister was supposed to pay a ton, enough for me to move across the country and cover four years of tuition at a state university with a strong radio astronomy program. Instead, I found myself caring for three humans—four, including me. I took classes on the internet and finally cobbled together an undergrad degree from an online college that Uri and Luce and Sulien had never heard of. I got a solid C average in all my classes, failed a few and had to retake them, but in the end slipped through. I did all the studying I could on my own to pass the test you need to become eligible to apply for radio astronomy programs.

Four times I have failed that test, but I am patient. As Sulien says, "Three years sitting on a rock." Luce says it's Sulien's way of telling me that good things come to those who wait.

Instead of three on a rock, I've spent seven years sitting in the driver's seat of Route 0. It's a zombie route. In order to retain state funding, we have to run at least three routes, but the other two are just as empty. When I started out, the routes were full, but then people started working online from home, and now there's no commute. Uri and I have money with the life insurance policy from his sister, but we're trying not to dip into that too much, trying to keep it so that when the time comes, the triplets can go to college.

After Luce leaves, I check on them again, find myself lulled into their room by the sounds of space. I sit in the rocking chair and listen until that satisfactory click that indicates the tape has run out. Then I press rewind, grateful to watch something move in reverse.

Sometimes when the triplets are asleep, I pull out the VCR and hook it up to the vintage TV and put on the videotapes from when my dad and Luce were little, let them run while I am busy paying the bills or cleaning the bathroom or looking through my cheap, third-hand telescope. It's only when the videos have ended that I sit down and settle in to watch, press rewind. Then it is everything regressing, swiftly: a very young Luce splashing out of the lake and landing dry on shore. A sandcastle meticulously unbuilt, until my father and Luce smooth the spot it was on. The tide going out as the day moves from evening to morning. The grandfathers I barely remember holding hands, kissing, hanging their children upside-down over the water, then placing them back on the ground, ankles first. My grandfathers picking up the empty beer cans scattered around them, raising them to each others' mouths, then placing them into the cooler. My tiny father and Luce waving at the camera, then walking backward until all four of them get into the truck, the whole day yet to come.

I am in the triplets' room, and I am thinking of the stars, how my memories of seeing them are fading. I am thinking of Saturn, the orb far above and the small cement block in the ground.

I will pass the test, I think then, and then I think of a heliospheric current sheet and its relationship to the sun.

I will pass the test, I whisper to myself. I will find a way to do it and in doing it be more. For myself. For the triplets. For my father.

I am in the triplets' room listening to space, and I am thinking of the nests and my father and the sky—how a person, like a bird, makes a home.

159

My grandfathers wanted to build worlds. They met at The Factory and got to talking on the production line about their shared love of atlases. Two years later, they were living together, and a year after that, my father and Luce were born. They bought a small house with a big garage which they turned into their studio and did artisan maps to order—the territory however small or large you wanted, and you could choose your color scheme. But what they really loved to make was the globes.

Luce lives in that house now, keeps her fathers' workshop in the garage in excellent condition. And while she knows all their secrets, having watched and listened to her fathers over the years, she herself has never tried her hand at the craft. She remembers the particular glue they used, the dimensions of the strips of map as they correlated to the diameter of the orb, the safe way to pierce the hole at the top and bottom—antipodals, she tells me, the exact opposite side of the world. And she remembers the unique aspect of my grandfathers' work: globe revision. For a fee, folks could return their artisan globes to be revised as national and geographic borders and names changed. They did globes in forty languages, physical and political, all made their specific way with thick paper they created themselves from re-cycled materials and then formed into orbs in a process that was half inspired by pottery shaping, half by papier-mâché.

Once—back before The Factory became The Farm—I asked her if she had ever thought about opening the workshop back up, trying to take what her fathers told her about their work and put it into practice.

"Not for me," she said. "I'm a line man at The Factory—all I know is how to go one way as far as it will take me. I don't know anything about things that are circular. Plus, no one needs globes anymore. Not with the internet. You can have an up-to-date portrait of the world by the minute." She had ashed then and rubbed her shaved head, clicked her tongue. "I mean, shoot, do you know the average lifespan of a globe?"

"I'm not sure I know what you are asking."

"How much time goes by before it starts to get old and out of date."

I breathed in very slowly, held my breath. I breathed out. "Thirty years?"

"Thirty years *ago* it was five years. Now? With The Crisis? It's got to be no more than six months."

If The Crisis has taught us anything, it has taught us that nothing is as it is for very long, that nothing long-term is stable.

"My fathers," Luce said then, "said revision was difficult. Emotionally, I mean. At that time, it was mostly the political globes that were hard, the borders and names of countries changing. They always talked about the invisible strife that came with those changes, the wars and loss and horror and struggle, but also the liberation and joy. For them, it was never just a name change or fixed border. They'd get to caring about what that change meant."

We were sitting on one of the workbenches she had lining the perimeter of the garage. Her leg was crossed, her ankle on her knee, and she picked at the fraying hem of her pants.

"Back then, the physical map changes only came in here and there. But now? Think of it. A peninsula becoming an island. That island vanishing. A coast cut in by a fraction of a fraction of an inch. I mean, the people. All that movement. That is, in fact, how Sulien's family came to be here—because their own town wasn't habitable anymore."

Sulien and I had never spoken about this fact, and it made me curious about his upbringing, how he chose to be YES or NO when his parents hadn't had to.

Luce went on. "What my fathers made clear to me—what I could never really wrap my head around—was the slippage. They knew they were just recording in three dimensions what the world already was, but to them, every time they'd revise, they felt like they were responsible. I can't imagine if they were still at it—if I'd taken over for them. It would be impossible to keep up. I just don't know if representing the world in three dimensions makes any sense at all anymore."

I looked around the workshop then, took in the place that still lived the same way it did the last time they were here. It was a kind of museum, a little surreal and a little disquieting, and it was Luce's idea of home.

"What would they have thought about the birds disappearing?"

Luce shook her head. "It would have disturbed them. Like you and me. But your father? He would have been broken in half."

I nodded, then I told her I had to leave. I took the labyrinthine path from the back garage to the front yard, walking through the field of globes that occupied the lawn of the house of my grandfathers. There were over 150 globes in all, and as I passed them, here and there I spun one on its axis.

When I reached the road and looked behind me, I remember it looked like an off-kilter galaxy, a vast field of planets, but all of them—every one—Earth, replicated over and over again. A galaxy composed of an infinite number of the exact same world.

158

Four days after the weaverbird nest goes up, on my first lap of Route 0, I round the Sixth and Division intersection and see another nest. After my shift is over, I head straight there, where Sulien is inspecting the work. It looks like it's made of mud or clay. Its shape is like a tree stump with a dip in the center, shallow like a spoon.

"It's so minimal," I tell him.

"Yes, well. No time. The albatross spent 95% of its life over the open sea."

Eventually, Sulien grows quiet, then he sits on the ground in front of the nest and looks up.

"Who is making them?" I ask him.

He shakes his head, but I can't tell if he didn't hear me or he doesn't care to answer the question.

He's in awe of what he sees, and I know it, I can read it in the language of his form. I want to ask him so very many things then, about his parents who aren't from this town, who had to leave theirs because it became uninhabitable. About his challenge in choosing between YES and NO. About how he is always telling me to speak up and voice what I'm thinking, despite the fact that he seldom does this himself. About his partner who was lost in the same way so many in our town are lost, to that gap in the mental healthcare system, the gap into which my father fell. I want to ask Sulien about how losing someone that way makes one porous to many forms of sorrow. I want to ask his advice for grieving.

"Birds," Sulien says then, just as I am preparing to speak, "moved about the world using unique forms of listening and observation. They could see light humans cannot see. They could hear sounds humans cannot hear. Birds could tap into the Earth's magnetic fields with a very unique solution in their eye. There are so many ways humans cannot sense the world and its complex, interconnected patterns. Now, without birds, we may never understand."

I don't say anything, but I feel the meaning of what he is saying sink into my mind. When something is lost, it is lost forever, he is telling me, and I am reading between the lines. I am trying hard to listen in new ways.

I want to ask him questions then, but I don't. Instead, I think of Ohm's law and Lenz's law and I leave him there, looking at the nest, and make my way toward Saturn.

157

ICARUS: [Testing out the wings for the first time.] Artifice is not endowed with ethics; we trust the hand that makes the art to make it with a heart.

156

When I reach Saturn, I am surprised to find myself full of a soft kind of joy. I had thought that once the secret had been revealed, the magic of knowing would dissolve. But instead it's only been enhanced and projected. Which, I am realizing now, is precisely how it has been with my studying. The first time, when I learned it all initially, it had been like opening a portal to enchantment. Physics is like that, coming to understand the world in which you operate has all these invisible rules that govern it, rules that you adhere to without ever knowing. Learning those truths has made the world wider, my personhood more capacious. I shouldn't be surprised, then, to find myself so moved and taken with Saturn, this small cement block, the blue fading such that whole parts are missing their color, the text so worn by weather that it's hard to make out.

I know all about astronomy and physics, but less when it comes to the raw facts of planets, so yesterday I visited the library, where the air conditioning is infinitely better than the box in our window at the duplex. At the library, I gathered what I could.

Saturn is the sixth planet from the sun. It has 146 moons. It is the farthest planet that can be seen with the naked eye, if you are in the right part of the world, a part of the world where there is no light pollution and smog.

Saturn orbits the sun once every twenty-nine years, which means Saturn has not made its way around the sun once since I was born.

A day on Saturn is just over ten hours.

Saturn is a little over one light hour away from Earth, which means if you were in part of the world where you could see Saturn with the naked eye, what you would be seeing is Saturn an hour ago.

I am in the middle of a field on the road that leads nowhere and I am trying to do a better job of listening. I am listening for the birds and the future and my town, trying to discern the right next step.

I won't drive the bus soon, but I will pass the test. And Uri will finish his play. And the triplets will grow and expand and become three unique people.

I don't know yet if I am a YES person or a NO person, but I know I must decide soon.

Though I can't see it, Saturn is in the sky, just over one light hour away.

But by some strange logic, Saturn is also right here with me, right here on Earth, and I lean down and reach out to touch it.

155

Uri is in his side of the duplex with the triplets and I am on the porch reviewing the laws of combustion when Luce pulls up and parks on the street in front of our porch. The length of her truck covers about the width of the front yard in its entirety.

When she gets out, she waves at me, then leans over the fence on her forearms and smiles at the ground. She hasn't lit a cigarette yet, which means she must have news.

"What is it?" I ask across the tiny yard. I am surrounded by my physics books and open notepads, flashcards of equations.

"That opening in management I told you about? It went through," she says. "I got it," and she puts her hands on her hips. "The promotion went through."

"The promotion went through!" I yell, and she opens the gate and walks toward me and I jump up, disrupting my study materials to shake her hand. Then she pulls me in for a quick bump on the chest, which is one of three ways Luce gives a hug.

She lights up a cigarette and I say it again loudly—The promotion went through!—and she nods and smiles at the ground, puts her cigarette out on the bottom of her shoe and discards the spent butt into half of a discarded globe that lives on our front porch for just this reason.

Then Uri comes out with the triplets tailing him and asks what all the yelling is about.

"The promotion—it went through," Luce says, and then the triplets start clapping and they make a ring around her, repeating the word over and over. The promotion. The pro. Motion the. Pro Motion The Pro. Motion. Thepro. Motion. The promotion.

Time seems to slow, and I wonder if it's my déjà vu coming on, but I've struggled with it for so long that I know the signs and this is different. Time slows and the bodies around me—the bodies of the people I care for—they slow, too, but the sound of the triplets quickens: The promotion, the promotion, thepromotionthepromotionthepromotion. The triplets continue to say it over and over and I sit down on the porch, trying to assess what is unfolding in my brain. It occurs to me that the way they are saying the word, repeated again and again, it's uncanny. They keep repeating it until it escapes feeling like a word at all, just noise without meaning. It's as though the word was once a narrow channel and with each repetition, it gets ever more gaping and ambiguous.

This could have gone on for three minutes or an hour, I can't tell. Finally, Luce crouches down and collects the triplets into a pile on the ground and they stop, instead squawking and squirming and snorting as they try to get out of her grip.

Reality seems to click back into place then, and I breathe deeply for a few moments to collect myself. I hear Uri asking about the details of the new position, and his voice in my head feels like a warm hug.

Luce picks one triplet up and the other two pull at her loose trousers. "I'll be in charge of one room of The Farm. Keeping an eye over all the hardware, managing the temperature control. Making sure all the invisible information the hardware transports gets to where it needs to be," she says, swapping out one triplet for another. "Hell of a lot more responsibility," she says, "but I'm up for it." Uri says congrats and she nods him her thanks. Then her brow furrows as she runs her finger along one of the wings adhered to his back, tells him they're in really bad shape.

I take the cigarette from Luce's mouth and help myself to a puff, then another, then a third.

I see Luce look at Uri. He looks at the ground.

"Well, shit," she says, "I'm sorry. Me celebrating when your job is as good as gone."

"No, no, don't worry. It's not that at all," I say. "Really, it's something different. But I do wish I knew when. It's the waiting that gets me, knowing every time I climb into the seat, it might be the last." I hand her cigarette back, but she waves it away and I take it for my own.

"Promotion," I say, still getting reacclimated to the world, to the word, feeling it in my mouth and in my brain, hearing myself say it as soon as I think it, amazed at this synthesis.

And Luce says, "*Promotion*. Late Middle English. From Old French and Latin, 'to move forward.'"

154

That night in bed, after a particularly bad bout of déjà vu, what I choose to imagine as I am trying to reach sleep is a murmuration of starlings, those birds that warped and wove a wave of themselves through the sky.

I will pass the test, I think. That is all there is.

Girl, bad, curse, bird, I whisper, over and over again, watching what is now gone in the world come alive inside my mind.

153

I am crossing off yet another day on my calendar, reworking my study schedule to speed up what I can cover in a day. There is the Copernican principle to comprehend and the Friedmann–Lemaître–Robertson–Walker metric to memorize, fluid statics and fluid kinematics and fluid dynamics to compare. The triplets are with Uri but

I am listening to their tape of space, the whooshing and whomping and thumping and shrill shrieks and low roars.

I will be a radio astronomer because I want it so much that the blood inside me aches. If you want something enough, in this world, in this town, I believe that you can get it. It's about hard work and real want. It's about never giving up. I have shared this with Luce and Uri and Sulien, and they don't think so. But I am of a different worldview. I grew up in a different world than them.

It was radio astronomy that introduced us to the idea of the Big Bang. Radio astronomy that initiated the understanding that there was a microwave radiating off of everything—planets, stars, meteors, comets—and someone asked where did it come from and someone else figured out that it came from the beginning, from the moment that everything began. The Big Bang was the one great cause, and everything after it became that cause's effect.

Nothing happens without something initiating it.

One time, when we were about eleven, The Only Person I've Ever Loved—who did not know that I loved her, since I myself did not know then, only realizing this after she had gone, long after she'd left this no-name town—she brought me a tape. Tapes were rare and hard to come by, having been abandoned for better tech, so I was surprised when she handed it over. I grabbed it from her and my hand was sweaty and she asked why and I shrugged because I did not know at the time what love was.

I saw that it wasn't rewound, so I stuck it in my tape player and we sat there, waiting for it to return to its start. I remember she had this huge bruise on her calf and I thought about her blood beneath her skin, the way it orbited her body, and then I thought about mine. She was sitting with her legs folded up under her and she scooched over to me—how was the carpet not burning her shins? I remember thinking—and then around behind me and the tape was still rewinding and she casually started drawing with her finger across my back. "Can you tell what I'm writing?" she asked, and I tried to concentrate on the words as they took shape. The letters were being impressed on my back and those letters were crafting words and despite how hard I concentrated, how hard I tried to synthesize the strokes into letters and then collect the string of letters into words and then synthesize the words into sentences, I couldn't feel what she was saying. I guessed a few times and she punched my shoulder, hard. "You are the absolute worst at this," she said. "I am giving you crucial information here, knowledge that is significant," she said. "Concentrate!" I felt what could have been *future* or could have been *failure*, and then the sound of the tape clicked off. The beginning had been reached.

She positioned herself so her back was up against mine, both of us looking opposite ways. She was looking at my father's bookshelf and I was looking out the window. And then she pressed play.

It was the most beautiful sound I'd ever heard, like space, but clearly kinder: the shrills were softer, the groans longer and less severe, the pulsing less like cracks and more like beats. But the relationship was clear. It was almost like the sound of space had been softened, the edges curved instead of sharp. I had known the sounds of space—I had studied them so intensely I believed I knew those sounds better than the sounds of Earth—and listening to this tape was almost eerie, like listening to a parallel world.

We let the whole tape play, until it reached the click that indicated the long thin ribbon had run out, and we didn't move. Then, our backs still touching, facing the opposite way, she said, "It's yours. You can keep it."

"Thanks, but what—I mean, what is it? Where is it coming from?"

She swung around and moved in front of me so we were looking at each other, sitting on her legs in that way that looked so uncomfortable.

"You can't tell." It was less a question and more a statement, her face a bit deflated. "I found it at a garage sale," she said, then returned to her position so our backs were touching again. "It's the ocean. It's a recording of the deepest known part of the sea. I thought it was whales at first, but turns out, it's icebergs. All that weeping and moaning? It's icebergs breaking apart."

Something deep inside me opened a little bit then, because of course. Of course space makes the sister sounds to the bottom of the sea. And I got to feeling that there was a very careful structure to so much, a structure so clear and balanced and patterned that I was completely incapable of instituting anything close to being called control. The world was just going to produce its patterns, let them unfold and intersect, let them take shape in massive, incomprehensible ways and ways very minor, very microscopic, and I was one of those patterns, and I had to simply let my life play out.

"You can have it," she said. "It's for you," she said, then pulled a book from the shelf, stretched her legs across my lap, and started to read.

I looked out the window and I felt the tears about to come. My father had been dead for two weeks, and a cardinal was there in the sill. I looked at that cardinal and it looked at me and then pecked the window twice, nodded, and flew off.

I remember thinking then that the only life I could imagine for myself was one in which I was a radio astronomer. It was that or nothing, I told myself. There was no other route.

I remember thinking then how coincidental it was that the book the Only Person I've Ever Loved pulled from the shelf was a novel— my father's favorite—based on a retelling of Girl in Glass Vessel.

152

"The magic of rehearsal," Uri is telling me, as he has halted his performance of the play on our porch because he has made a mistake, "is that you can literally turn back time. You can erase the error and pretend it never happened. You can be forgiven by the act of expunging what you have just done wrong."

Later, I ask Luce the etymology of *rehearsal*. "That's a tricky one," she says. "It means repeat, of course, but its root word—*hearse*—comes from the Latin for turn over, or overturn, as in the soil, as in to prepare for burial. It also once meant a latticework canopy or frame one puts over a coffin."

When I watch Uri rehearse, I see him misspeak, slip up a line, get the blocking wrong. And then time is turned over, overturned. Time is erased and he rewinds, and I am so used to him moving this way—pausing, then correcting himself, moving forward again—that I realize I'm not sure if this is part of Icarus's nervous persona or if it's Uri messing up.

This is, to some extent, how I study—a misidentified term or error in an equation. But astronomy isn't narrative, so I cannot turn back time. I am marked by the mistake and I worry I'll reproduce it. I worry I'll remember what I failed at instead of what is true.

"From the beginning," Uri says, and I watch him stop the play in the middle and start it all over again.

151

The twelfth nest goes up near the library. I notice on the last loop of my route, as I'm trying to remember the star cluster Pleiades—the shape it made and where it lived this time of year. When I see the nest, I am disgruntled it took me all day to notice and remind myself of the importance of looking more closely. This is another lesson of The Crisis: look at and listen to and truly feel the world, because it will not be as it is for long.

When my shift is done, I walk the long way home past the library to see it up close. It's formed of thick grass as tall as cornstalks split in the middle and curved at the top so that the grass meets just above my head and interlaces together like a person folds their hands.

Scattered around the entrance are bits of refuse and garbage, all a bright shade of blue. I hear someone behind me approaching, and then I hear Sulien say, "The nest of the satin bowerbird."

"What's with the litter?" I ask Sulien, using my foot to create space between a large Tupperware lid, a thick and knotted cord of severed rope, and part of a car's bumper—all the color of the triplets' eyes.

"It's decoration. Bowerbirds collected natural material and arranged it by color to attract a mate. Orange, yellow, white. Satin bowerbirds focused exclusively on bright blue, but because it's rare in nature, they often used human garbage."

We are quiet then, as we stand in awe of the now-lost world of birds. I am partial to silence, have studied it just like I've studied sound, and so I know that silence with Sulien is like no other silence because it is full. But I also have to wonder about all that goes unsaid between us when there is so much to say—so much we could say to each other if only we tried.

Sulien sighs. "Did you know," he says to me, still looking at the nest, "that I have one of your grandfathers' globes?"

I can't hide my surprise, and Sulien knows it. He knows this about me.

"My mother gave it to me when I was very young. She was a wonderful person," he says, and I look at the ground because I've heard this from Luce, "and I am grateful I have this one thing. It is in her first language, a language I knew as a child but don't remember anymore, so I can't read it. But every night before bed, I spin it and listen to the soft revolutions as I fall asleep," he says.

He uses the tip of his toe to touch a bit of the human garbage before him, the garbage that is part of the satin bowerbird nest.

"I have never had it revised," he says. "It's like a time capsule that way, an artifact. But I feel I owe it to her to get it revised. Your grandfathers revised her own globe so very many times over the years. And so I wonder," he says. "I wonder—if I asked her—I wonder if Luce would revise it."

It feels like something is opening then, like a door has been cracked, just a bit, and we are on either side. The door is still between us, but there's a space now, for us to speak into and to hear through. Sulien has never shared this much with me before, despite the fact that I tell him everything.

"She doesn't do globes," I tell him. "Says she doesn't know how to work in circles."

Sulien uses his foot to move the blue car bumper, looks up at the top of the nest. "How would you suggest we change her mind?"

150

I once asked Luce if she preferred a different pronoun. It was before I'd failed the test the first time. We were sitting on my porch, and the bottom of the globe of cigarette butts was getting full. I remember thinking I should dump it out.

She huffed a laugh and said if she wanted another pronoun, she would make it known. "It's not that the one I have fits," she said then, using her thumb to press away some smudge on the side of her boot, something she must have picked up at The Factory, back before there was The Farm. "It's not that it fits. It's just that I've gotten used to it and you know how I feel about change." Then she smiled a sad smile and half shoved and half pressed her shoulder into my side until I almost fell over, which is one of three ways that Luce gives a hug.

149

The triplets, Uri, and I are lying on the grass in our tiny front yard, looking up at the swirling clouds of smog. Uri has dragged me from my room where I've been studying for the last four hours, my eyes red and raw from reading the screen, my textbooks, my notes. He pulled me outside and asked that I look at the world around me, above me. You are working too hard, he said, and I said I had no other choice, and he looked at me like Luce did in the weeks after my father died, like I was wearing a cloak of pain, and in that moment I chose to give in. We are lying in the yard now trying to find meaning in the shapes above us, but the clouds look only like waves or collections of dust. We cannot see castles in the air.

I can hear the sound of Luce's truck from a mile away. When she parks in front of our duplex a minute later, it feels like I willed it to happen, like she'd been planning to go elsewhere, but I'd used my hope to pull her here right now.

Luce slams the door too hard, and the triplets, all three of them at once, stand up and run over to the fence. She leans over it and tussles the hair on each of their heads.

She lights a cigarette, then yells for Uri.

"Come here a minute. Let me see those wings," Luce says. Uri walks over in character, Icarus's nervous gait. "They're getting awfully beat up. Snags in the nylon, holes everywhere. Did you see this? How the frame is all bent on this side? No, these won't do at all."

Then Luce pulls out from the cab of her truck a stunning set of intricately woven wire wings. They are breathtaking, the way the wire lattices weave and morph into each other, looking like feathers, the complexity of the metalwork. She's attached a harness to the back.

She comes through the front fence and into the yard.

"All recycled material," she says. "I had to guess at the size, used Sulien as a blueprint, but it's got to be close."

Uri puts them on and they fit perfectly. His face looks suddenly, blindingly new.

"Thinking was," Luce says, "you can fit things inside the wire's weave. Bits of fabric and feathers and the like but also notes and other decoration. That way you can really make them yours. The right ending will come to you soon, but I figured these might help."

One of the Triplets brings over a leaf and Another of the Triplets offers a piece of crayon. Luce tucks each into Uri's wings and Uri moves around a bit and they stay firmly rooted in place.

Uri very slowly wraps his arms around Luce and she lets him for a fraction of a second, then says, huffing but with a smile, "Okay, all right," and tries to wiggle out, but Uri holds her tighter until she gives up. She doesn't hug him back, but she is still and she is smiling and shaking her head and then they break away from each other. Uri holds her shoulders when he silently mouths the words *thank you* and Luce nods and blows smoke out of her nose.

That night I visit Saturn and I bring tools. I carve away the earth around it, this faded and chipped blue cement block, until the sharp edges of the four corners are visible. Then I use my pocketknife and an old toothbrush and clean up the indentations that compose the sixth planet's name and rings.

It doesn't look as good as new, not even close, but that is not the point. What it looks is better. It looks like someone cares.

On the way home, I walk toe to heel and review the major causes of Johnson–Nyquist noise which is really just electronic disturbance. It isn't noise at all.

148

The next morning, the triplets ask what a bird sounded like, and the hair on my arms stands straight up.

I ask Uri for access to the crawlspace—the crawlspace is on his side of the duplex, the attic is on mine—and I pull out the boxes of my old tapes, then the shoebox labeled BIRDS and flip through the tapes a few times until I come to one that says, in my father's handwriting, GRAY CATBIRD. I take the triplets to the front porch and sit them in a circle and put in the tape but of course it isn't rewound—nothing in my life seems rewound—and while we wait for the tape to get to its beginning, the triplets tell me that light cannot escape a black hole. I nod slowly and swallow twice and wonder where they are getting this information. Then we hear the click that the tape is rewound and I set the player in the middle of the triplets and push play.

The sound fills me with strangeness. I am partial to strangeness, but this feels truly dreamlike, since I know this sound is no longer unfolding in my backyard, in my town, in my community. Since the triplets will never hear this sound at all but from recordings. It is a catbird, locked into the past, doomed to repeat this ephemeral call, these songs, for eternity, as long as someone is there to rewind the tape and press play. We listen to the bird, and the song is long and it doesn't repeat much and we let this sound enter our bodies through our ears.

The sound the bird makes is like an encryption, like it is telling us something in Morse code. There is no pattern—it is all just chaotic chirps and whistles—but the rhythm it makes sounds to me exactly like the rhythm of a human's fingers on a keyboard typing.

We sit there listening, and the triplets are perfectly still. Their eyes are closed, trying to imagine, I am betting, this animal in the real world. We stay that way for the full duration of the tape and when the tape is done, the triplets ask for another.

I shuffle through the tapes again. The sound of the plastic cases hitting each other is superb. I pull one out. In my father's handwriting, I show the triplets—who cannot read—the label which says: MAGPIE.

This tape isn't rewound either, but the triplets sit patiently through this process and then the click indicates it's done and before I can reach into their circle, One of the Triplets hits play.

There is the long song of the bird, a few calls. It sounds to me like there is something akin to sorrow in it, but I stop myself. Sulien would tell me not to anthropomorphize.

And just as I'm trying to think of another way to characterize what the magpie's song feels like, something happens on the tape. We start to hear something disturbing, something uncomfortable. The bird who is singing to us through time, that bird's song starts to mimic the sounds that humans make.

There is the sound of a chainsaw, then the sound of an ambulance. The sound of a motorcycle.

Then, to my horror, there is the sound of a laughing child.

It is distinct, clear to all of us, and we look at each other with faces that convey our discomfort. I reach out to turn the tape off, but One of the Triplets grabs my arm.

We listen to the tape. The triplets hear the human world through this bird. They listen the whole way through, but this time, they keep their eyes open.

When the tape stops, all three of them stand up and tell me they are done with listening for today. Then they ask what kind of noise a black hole makes.

147

URI: Should we tell her? That even if she passes this fifth time, which she won't, she still has a million hurdles? That she barely even passed the classes to get her that online degree? Should we tell her it's not going to happen?

LUCE: I've thought about it. I almost did it once. Twice. So yes, maybe we should. But Uri—even if we wanted to—that time I almost did—I couldn't. Because I had no idea—no conception at all—about how to do it. Even if we wanted to tell her, Uri—how would we do it? So she listened? How could we make her hear?

146

The Only Person I've Ever Loved used to look up at the sky before a storm and say, "Looks like we're going to get weather."

She would be biting her nails—she was always biting her nails—and I would pull her hand from her mouth, remind her to be good to herself.

"Looks like we're going to get weather," she'd say, but I always found it strange because weather is ongoing. Weather is always. At every moment of every day weather is unfolding. For some reason, she only called it weather when it looked bad.

I think of weather, the scale of it, how big it is. How even with all our advances, we still can't predict it.

One of the last times I saw her, just before she left for good, I watched her look up at the sky and I said, "There's no more wonder in the world. Humans have figured everything out. Weather might be man's last mystery."

She looked at me then with a face of concern and started biting again. "You're wrong," she said, spitting out a bit of nail. "Man's last mystery is death."

145

Luce has dragged me away from studying and now we're in the bed of her truck, outside my side of the duplex, listening to the baby monitor convey to us what is happening in the triplets' room. I have two months left until the test. What we hear is space.

"How was The Rally this week?" Luce asks.

"We call it The Demonstration now," I tell her.

"Sure. The Demonstration."

"There were two sides," I tell her, "and I was on one of them."

Luce lets out a grunt which is her way of laughing. "Seems that's how it will always be."

"I need to get back to studying," I tell her.

"You need to spend time in the world. You need to spend time with your face in the world. With your heart and your feet in the world," she responds.

"I'm in the world," I say, "I'm in the world studying."

"Seems to me that you're in some prospective future. You're not in the present. In this singular now."

I am quiet for a moment, thinking about the test. I wish then we were in her yard, and I transport myself there in my head and imagine standing in the galaxy of Earths, the breeze spinning a few of the globes. Then I ask her why she thinks she loves etymology.

"Don't love etymology, per se. Just find it useful to track things back. Especially words. With their meaning always changing—sometimes it's useful to remember their roots."

"Hmm," I say.

"Plus, I find I use a word differently after I know where its meaning came from. I find myself reflecting on the fact that these are words folks used thousands of years ago, that the words I'm saying now, they came from the mouths of folks going back centuries, but those words are living still. I'm a factory man," she says, "and I come from a line of factory men. I prefer in this life to use my hands. But all of us—every one—we all use words." Luce ashes over the side of the truck. "Seems to me in some ways words is all we are," she says, and her face goes blank, as though when she hears herself say it, she finds she believes it, too.

I stare at Luce then and watch her thinking to herself and I wonder about the way she is so unknown to me, even as she's the closest thing I now have to a parent. She is always reaching toward some larger, grander notion of life. It's like Uri, and like Sulien, but the absolute opposite of me. I'm grateful for the help of those around me, but I'm often intimidated by how much they all think. I myself am much better at feeling.

Perhaps this is why I continue to fail the test.

She is still staring into some portal of meaning that I cannot access and I look at her and I shudder for a minute because I transpose the face of my father just before his death over hers and I see it: it's him, he's alive and has aged, and he's sitting next to me.

When she speaks, the illusion dissolves.

"I'm not much for books and art and such—you know that—but etymology, that is something I understand. Something I can wrap my hands and head around. Everything has an invisible past."

My impulse is to rewind things, to track things back, and I wonder then if the source of that impulse is inherited. Perhaps, even, it is linked with my déjà vu.

"I'll let you in on a secret," Luce says. "Can't tell another soul."

I nod.

"When my fathers would revise a globe, they would tell their clients they had removed everything in that world that was out of date. But they didn't actually cut out the old version and replace it." She leans in close, whispers. "When they revised a globe, they'd leave the previous layer there and put the new strip of map—with the adjusted border or new name of the country or the revised coastline—they'd put that new strip over it. Felt wrong to just cut out what once was and get rid of it. The new layer is what is visible, but they'd always know the truth: that everything which has come before has left a trace on that sphere, invisible but present."

I gather, slowly, that she is also, to some extent, talking about etymology.

Luce has put out her cigarette. While I have been listening, she has used the tip of her finger to line her spent ones up. Then she takes one hand and swoops all of them into the upside-down northern hemisphere of a flawed globe, her makeshift ashtray. She turns up the volume on the baby monitor and lies down in the bed of the truck, looks at the light-polluted sky.

"Not much for art," she says, "but etymology—that makes sense to me."

I realize that I don't believe her when she says this, because she made Uri's wings.

We get quiet then, listening to the sounds of space from forty years ago, through a tape recording playing upstairs, through a baby monitor sitting next to us.

I think of equations and laws and principles. I think of physics. But I also think of stories, of Icarus, Chicken Little, Girl in Glass Vessel. It's amazing to me how humans have found such marvelous and magical ways to trap and then hold onto things, ways to take what should be fleeting and never let it go.

144

ICARUS: *[In bed, anticipating the best way to follow the middle path.]* No, yes. Yes, no. Yes, yes. No. No. Yes, no, no, yes. Yes, yes. No.

143

Before the triplets were born, when I was still a surrogate and before I'd become a legal guardian, Uri's sister and her partner asked me over to their home for cake. I accepted and brought them one of my grandfathers' flawed globes. It had been mounted upside down.

They liked the globe and I ate three pieces of cake and they asked me why I'd chosen to do this. They were nervous to ask, I could see, but I could also see that they were sincere, and I had nothing to hide.

I told them I needed the tuition for school so I could become a radio astronomer. I told them, too, that I had spent my life struggling to hear but that it really wouldn't matter so much since radio astronomy is more about math than sound.

This seemed to be a good answer to them, and they packaged up the rest of the cake and sent me on my way with it. But before they did, they leaned down to my stomach and spoke to the triplets. I covered my ears so as to give them privacy, and when they stood up they were crying.

I handed them the handkerchief Luce had given me, the one with a tiny globe embroidered in the corner, and they passed it back and forth.

"It's just—" Uri's sister said, before I knew Uri. Before I knew she had a brother at all. "We're so very grateful," she said. "Thank you so much," she said, and I nodded and left with the cake.

On the walk home, I reflected on what I was doing, which until then I had tried pretty hard not to do. I was a gestational surrogate, which meant that the humans inside me were not in any way related to me genetically—the egg and the sperm both belonged to this couple, and I was merely the flesh shell in which the triplets were being incubated. I reflected on that, thought briefly that maybe I'd visit in a decade or two, after I'd learned to understand space, pop in for an eighteenth birthday or a wedding or a family reunion. Uri's sister and her partner seemed like the kind of people who would be okay with that. Then, the cake growing warmer in my arms since the afternoon was balmy, I remembered the contract we had signed all those months ago, remembered Uri's sister's handwriting on the bottom of the contract—she'd signed it and then wrote in tiny blue ink, "You don't know what this means."

Except, at the time, she was wrong. I absolutely did. I knew precisely what it meant.

Last week I tried to look for that contract, to see Uri's sister's handwriting at the bottom of the page, but I couldn't find it. I searched everywhere, asked Luce to look, too, and even Uri. And then, three days into my hunt, I thought something really surreal. I wondered if I'd made it up, if there hadn't been a contract at all.

Uri once said the function of fiction is to illuminate a truth. It's a paradox, he said.

But I guess so is being born knowing you will die and choosing to live anyway.

Whether or not the contract existed, I have a memory of Uri's sister writing that somewhere. Maybe on a napkin or a postcard. Maybe on the back of a photograph. Maybe in the memo line of a check.

You don't know what this means, she wrote, and it's only now that I believe her.

142

"This can't be right," I am saying to Sulien. He crosses his arms, tilts back on his heels to take in the majesty of the nest before us.

"There's no way a bird could do this," I am telling him, and he smiles, which informs me I'm wrong.

"The nest of the common tailorbird. Named so for obvious reasons."

The nest is tall and deep and constructed of some kind of false fabric made to look like leaves. They are green and teardrop shaped, and where they come together—I can barely believe my eyes—there, the leaves have been sewn.

"The base of the nest is a collection of hard sticks, but outside, for camouflage and protection, the tailorbird sewed itself a kind of curtain with leaves."

"How did it make the thread?" I ask.

"The webbing from spiders or the fiber from plants. Then it used its beak to poke a hole in the leaf, and threaded the strands through, back and forth and back and forth again."

What is catching me off guard is how human it looks. The stitch is a zigzag and it's imperfect, which makes sense—this was work that needed to happen quickly in order to lay the eggs. It's the flaws and defects, the way the holes for the fiber thread aren't perfectly aligned, the way there are a few extra stitches where the leaf has split, that flusters me.

"On average, it took four days and up to two hundred stitches."

"Did the bird learn that from humans or the other way around?" I ask Sulien.

"No one knows, but I think it was the other way around," he says. "Very long ago," he says, and then he sighs loudly and whispers, "Once upon a time."

141

I am studying in my room—tonight it's spectral density—and I can hear the triplets talking to themselves through the wall and then I hear them all saying *the sky is up, the sky is up, the earth is down, the earth is down* in unison, and it is a bit creepy, but also somehow quaint because it is so obvious and true. And it is then that I remember the day I realized the stars were gone.

The Only Person I've Ever Loved and I were in the field—the very field where I would, years later, find Saturn—as this was the best place to stargaze. We'd made the trek out there for seven days straight and hadn't seen a thing. I'd been busy with one of my father's worst episodes for the previous two weeks, staying at Luce's and helping out in the ways that I could while she was tending her twin at our apartment. I'd do laundry and hang it on the line, wash the windows, sweep and vacuum, pour cans of food into bowls to heat up in the microwave whenever she eventually made her way home. I was eleven. I loved the stars, but my life—the life I was trying to forge with my father—was complicated and I hadn't had time to meet with The Only Person I've Ever Loved, nor did I have time to visit the field where the stars were at their best during that difficult stretch.

"It's been a whole month without stars," she told me.

"You mean a week. We've only failed to come out here for a few days in a row. Some weeks are cloudier than others."

"It's been a month. While you were—" and she sort of waved her hand, since we did not talk about my father, did not talk about his mental health or the way this town's gap in healthcare meant he couldn't get the help he needed, that he had to rely on Luce and I— she waved her hand to signal what would not be said, then proceed- ed—"during that time, I came here every night. You've been gone longer than you think."

I became a bit sweaty then, a bit rattled, and I pulled my binocu- lars back up to my eyes, continued to scan the sky.

A month, two more, and then I had to admit she was right. While I did not yet realize the scope of the situation, it was that night in the field when I came to understand the not-so-slow crawl of change.

This is often how things end, I have since come to learn—every- thing is really a process. There are seldom tidy conclusions, a blunt goodbye and then the closing of the book. It is always gradual, a creeping, and you can't discern until sometime later, when the end is confirmed, just right where the end began. It's only in the retrospec- tion that you can start to map out how things got as bad as they got, only in hindsight how X links up with Y, how One Day was The Day it started going downhill.

This is how it was with the birds, a few of them spotted here or there after that strange act of them—all different kinds—flocking together. This is how my father's mental health got so bad that it started to affect him physically; I did not realize it was happening until it was too late.

This is how it's been with The Crisis, as we linger on its precipice.

The birds are gone—that's clear—but the stars.

Like the layers of my grandfathers' globes, I still hold out hope that we can peel away the artificial coatings to reveal what lies behind all the light pollution and dirty clouds.

Which is, of course, the rest of the universe.

140

The problem, Uri is telling me again, is The End. We're drinking beer in our front yard—a break from studying for me—and the wings Luce made him are drooping. I reach over to fix them. He wiggles his shoulders a bit to help me, shaking his head at the ground.

"Look there," I say, pointing up above to a smear of hazy sky. "Given this time of year, without the smog, right there is where Venus would be."

He looks up, tries to use his gaze to follow the line of my arm.

"What got you into space to begin with?" he asks.

I take another deep swig. "I guess my father and Luce. My grandfathers indirectly, since I barely remember them. My grandfathers had all these maps and atlases that seemed to live everywhere, and when I was little, I would think: who can see the world this way? Who gets to be up and above, to see the world that I know so intimately from so far away, so that everything becomes tiny, infinitesimal? The answer, of course, being astronauts."

"Or birds," Uri says, and my breath catches in my chest.

He raises his beer in the air. "'The flight paths of the past, though spectral, frame the future,'" he says. It's the line that opens Act 2.

I raise my beer, too, then drink deep and lie back on our blanket. "The night we buried my father, this strange thing happened. I didn't know it then, but I later learned it's a rare occurrence at twilight when it's cold out. The light refracts against the ice crystals and that, mixed with air pollution, makes the sunset illuminate the rising moon."

He shifts his shoulders to adjust his wings. "I'm not sure I understand," he says.

"Two suns." I sit up and take another swig. "The sky looks like it has two suns."

"'Somewhere in the cosmos, Earth's twin reveals our mirror-lives,'" Uri says. It's from the middle of Act 3, when Daedalus is fastening the wings on Icarus.

I don't know what to say so I say nothing. I think of eggs and wings and feathers and nests. Then he mumbles to himself, "Two suns," polishes off his beer, kisses my forehead, and leaves me for his side, which is the opposite of my side, the world turned inside out.

139

I decide to take a practice test, to see how I am progressing. This, I think, will give me a sense of where I'm at. I download it online and print it at the library and then I ask Uri to take the triplets for the evening, and he makes me a big meal and I set the timer to complete the test within the allotted five hours, with a twenty-minute break right in the middle.

I had Luce print off the answers, and now Uri is comparing my answers to the key while I wait upstairs, lying in my bed, my star charts above me. In the middle of the ceiling is the chart with my father's handwriting in the corner, noting the date of the eclipse.

My father had been ill since before I was born. Depression, anxiety, agoraphobia. Then: insomnia, panic attacks, hallucinations. All this had been hurting him in small and large ways for much longer than the span of my life.

It was a heart attack that did it in the end. The illnesses accumulated and coalesced and amplified each other, worked on his body for so long his heart couldn't hold out.

Luce and I tried to get help. He was in and out of the hospital and always between doctors, but no one knew just what was wrong. Or rather, the network of things meant no one knew where to begin. His heart palpitations could have been his anxiety, his bowel issues his depression. Was he getting exercise and eating right? The doctors wanted to know. But they didn't know how to interpret my answers: he is scared to leave the house, refuses sunlight. He has not gotten out of bed for four days, refuses food. He will not speak. He cannot sleep. We'd get prescriptions for antidepressants and antipsychotics and a date for a return visit, but none of this ever worked. No one could help us because no one knew how to deal with the web of what was wrong.

He would say these things, these things that horrified and gutted me, these things that made me hurt for him so much that it felt like my own body was carrying his pain.

What if, he would say, the people I believe are harmless turn out to want to hurt me.

What if, he would say, time isn't real and every moment you are living happens infinitely. What if this right now is infinite, this sorrow. What if my sorrow is infinite.

He would do this for days and Luce and I would call the doctor and there would be nothing they could do. Eventually, with coaxing from Luce, he would get himself to a point where he could drag himself to The Factory to make up for his missed shifts. A month later, he'd be back in his bed refusing to eat, wondering aloud these devastating things.

What if, he would say, I look nothing like what I imagine and the fact of seeing me as I see myself is actually an evolutionary form of protection, veiling my own true hideousness. What if that hideousness cannot be escaped.

What if when I look in the mirror, I do not have a face.

What if my food is poisoned, my clothes are poisoned, the walls of my home are poisoned. What if my skin is poisoned and I need to take it off to save myself.

What if you do not exist. You, my daughter, what if you do not exist. What if I have imagined you.

I exist, I would tell him, the core of me both frozen and molten hot. I exist, I would say and run the cool towel over his chest.

On his worst days, he would say the worst things, and these are the days I'd get Luce. Eventually these days became more regular. When

Luce realized how bad it had gotten, she took me to her house and I stayed there while she tended to him. She would make me dinner and tuck me into bed, then go over to our apartment to do the work of being a twin to him, the kind of work she never discussed with me.

She knew what I was going through, but she was careful about the way she handled it. The way she handled it was like this: she fed me and clothed me and gave me books to read. She gave me chores to do, tasks to accomplish. She slowly took all my star charts off the wall of my father's apartment and put them in his childhood room, the room in the house she had inherited, the room that would become mine after he died.

So many ailments faced by the people in our town had a clear answer, a bridge from diagnosis to treatment to recovery. But for my father, and for Luce and I, there was an abyss and we had no bridge from his illnesses to getting him well.

Uri knocks on my door and hands me a piece of paper. I hold my breath for a moment as he stands there at the entrance to my room, his wings filling up the doorway. Then he hangs his head. I have failed the practice test.

"The rehearsal," he tells me, "is not the performance." He hands me the sheet of paper noting which questions I got wrong, as well as the test and the key. Then he shuts my door.

I flip to a new page of my notebook, clear the marks from my dry erase board. The first question I got wrong is the first question of the test.

The rehearsal is not the performance. There is still time. Labor and desire, I think then. All it takes is work and want.

138

By the time I get home from my shift on Route 0 for the day, Luce is already outside sitting in the bed of her truck, spent cigarettes lining the ledge. I climb in and thank her for watching the triplets, especially since it isn't her day—Uri had asked for some time to himself to tackle his new ending.

"A fourteenth nest has gone up," I tell Luce, and she raises her eyebrows, puts out her cigarette. She squints into the distance.

"Will he ever finish?"

I light my cigarette and take a drag. "Uri or whoever's putting up the nests?"

"What I don't get," Luce says, ignoring my question and picking a bit of loose tobacco from her tongue, "is that he's chosen mimicry. The story he's telling—it's already been told. Seems to me the end's been written."

We both shrug and shake our heads and it is a moment of mutual recognition that there are things about the world that we do not understand, not for lack of interest, but because they can't be known.

"How was The Rally—sorry, The Demonstration this week?"

"There were two sides," I say, and she interrupts me.

"—and you were on one of them."

"Do you remember participating?"

"'Course. Been going on as long as this town has existed. Your father and I—our fathers were both for NO, so we spent most of our time there when we came of age. But others had it harder. We had a childhood friend whose mother was a NO and father was a YES. She struggled for almost a year to decide. And then take Sulien, for example," she shakes her head, pulls at the unraveling hem of her pants. "His family came here from another town, once theirs became uninhabitable. His parents never had to choose themselves, so he had to figure it out on his own. Aside from learning a new language and new laws in a new town, there was this custom that he had to participate in. He was the first in his family to have to do it. From what he has told me, it was hard."

I nod.

"Imagine," she says. "When they are young adults, the triplets will participate."

I cringe, but turn my head first so she doesn't see. "Maybe it will be over by then."

"Used to think that myself," Luce says. "But these days I wonder if it's simply in the blood of this town to disagree."

I can hear Uri's voice through the open window, reciting the scene when Icarus is standing on the windowsill of the tower, imagining the act of taking flight. Yes, no, no, yes, Icarus says, trying to find the middle path.

"You know what Uri told me today?" Luce says. "Said storywriting—novels and the like—came out of drama, from what he called the soliloquy. Said the monologue—which is all about speaking to the self, or to god, or the audience, which is supposed to be invisible to everyone on stage—just kind of jumped out of the play world and onto the page when everyone became literate. Monologues got longer and deeper and could be understood privately since everyone could read, so rather than getting that insight into another's mind by watching someone perform it, folks just picked up a book."

Aunt Luce rubs her shaved head, sighs.

"Makes you think, huh? I mean, sometimes," she lights a new cigarette, "sometimes I get to feeling I myself have an ongoing story I'm telling inside my head. A story about myself that I'm narrating all the time, every day. Makes me wonder," she says. "I wonder," she says, and lets her thoughts trail off with the smoke.

"About what? What do you wonder?" I ask.

"Who it is I'm speaking to," she says, and she looks me directly in the eye.

It feels like she is trying to tell me something then, like she is trying to will me to know something about the world or myself that I don't know yet. I want to make her proud, but I don't see it—this thing she wants me to know. I've gotten this sense from Uri before, too, and once from Sulien. Whatever it is, it's invisible to me, as opaque as whether or not I am a YES or NO person.

Three years sitting on a rock. Everything will come in time, I think then, and suddenly I am overcome with a really intense bout of déjà vu.

137

Once, on a Saturday at the library, The Only Person I've Ever Loved and I overheard the librarian reading to a group of children a really interesting version of Girl in Glass Vessel. My father was already gone, so we must have been twelve or thirteen. We'd hid between the stacks, lying on the ground, and we didn't talk the whole time, just listened to the man's deep voice convey the story, listened to the gentle wisp of the pages as they turned. For both of us it had been the first time in a long while that someone had read to us and while we would not admit it to each other, we found it tapping into something ancient and forgotten. Perhaps it was the memory of being inside a womb, listening to all the sound unfolding in the world outside our flesh shell, the world we'd yet to meet but knew was there.

When the story was over, The Only Person I've Ever Loved sighed and said, "The thing about Girl in Glass Vessel stories—the thing that gets me, is the end."

"Why the end?" I asked her.

"Oh, you know," she said, beginning to bite her nails. "Girl in Glass Vessel stories don't really have one."

I'd never thought about the story like that until this point, until The Only Person I've Ever Loved put it that way.

Then, suddenly, she winced and sucked in her breath and pulled her hand away from her mouth, squeezed her finger. She'd bitten her nail down to the quick and beyond, and her finger was covered in blood.

"The things you do to yourself," I said then, shaking my head and pulling her toward the bathroom.

The things we do to ourselves, I remember thinking that afternoon as we were waiting for the bus to take us home. I remember thinking that and then thinking of my father and looking at her, The Only Person I've Ever Loved, except at the time I didn't know I loved her.

The bus was running late and in the distance, I remember, I could hear the voices of the young adults in our town at The Demonstration yelling NO and YES. I remember I listened really carefully but no matter how hard I tried, I couldn't tell which side's voices were louder.

136

I am crossing today off my calendar when I realize that the test is exactly one month away. For a moment I get sweaty, then I get resolved. I will pass the test, I tell myself, over and over. I run this through my head as I'm dressing the triplets, adjusting my seat on the bus, eating the meals Uri makes me each night. I have worked harder preparing for this test than I have the others. Cumulatively, I know more than I ever have. I will pass the test, I think. There is no alternative.

I am in bed now, looking up at my star charts, thinking I need to pull myself up and out, need to get back to studying. My eyes hurt every morning, every night, and I dream of equations floating in and out of the air above me.

I dream, too, of The Only Person I've Ever Loved.

Sometimes, I reflect on how much of my life I've spent waiting for audio tapes to rewind, all that time I have waited for ribbons of sound to return—and I wonder if anyone else who is of my generation has spent this much time moving backward in order to move forward again.

I have not seen The Only Person I've Ever Loved since she left our no-name town, left without telling me one evening and never returned. We were seventeen.

When she left, of course, I did not know I loved her. I only found out when she was gone. I am usually a bit late to knowing myself.

I wait for her return, which I know will happen one day. And though I don't believe we'll love each other then, don't believe we will find a way to suture our lives together like the nest of the tailorbird, what I hope for is that she will visit one last time in order to tell me goodbye. Perhaps in order to tell me she's sorry for leaving me behind.

In the meantime, I remain human. Which is to say that there have been other women. There have been other women in my bed. There have been women and there have been men. In my bed and theirs.

I remain human, so there have been naked limbs and skin touching; there has been sweat. Before the triplets and after. There has been intimacy, and there has been lust, but there has never been love.

I have done the things it takes to keep my desire satiated with hes and shes and theys. But with The Only Person I've Ever Loved, there wasn't even a kiss.

Sometimes I wonder if that means I couldn't love her.

Other times I wonder if a kiss would break the spell.

Uri says that the thing about yearning is that as soon as it is satisfied, it finds a way to disappear. This is why, Uri says, the ending must be inevitable but also surprising, so that it both fulfills the audience's expectations and also subverts them. So that you give them closure but also keep them hovering on the edge of possibility even after the curtain is closed.

There have been hims and hers and thems, but at night, in the dark, when I'm alone, I rewind to the past and when it's done, when I'm at the beginning, there is one person, always: The Only Person I've Ever Loved.

135

SULIEN: Do you ever wonder why it is that you want what you want?
LUCE: All the time. Every day. *[Beat.]* I think it has to do with what ideas you inherit.
SULIEN: Why do you think people want things that hurt them?
LUCE: Sulien. You're talking like people are in control of their desire.
SULIEN: It just strikes me that longing is a guise, beneath which something is always hidden.
LUCE: Everyone has the right to wish.
SULIEN: Everyone has the right, but I wonder if we should try harder to wish responsibly.

134

There are twenty days until my test. I do my rounds on Route 0 and think of my future, a future anchored to space. Above me at night, my star charts map out the sky, a sky I don't recognize when I look outside.

We knew our town was in the path of totality many years before the eclipse came. These are the kinds of things that can be determined decades in advance, the kind of things that made me want to work with the stars. Some aspects of the future can be known, and it's all math, and that fact, to me, is mesmerizing.

I remember my father telling me when I was young that the eclipse would be unfolding in the future and that our town would be in the path of totality. This was long before the birds had disappeared, when we could still see the stars. Everything seemed stable and possible, and the future seemed full.

He told me how old I would be when it came and how people would travel from all over the continent to our town in anticipation of seeing the event. He told me I would be a radio astronomer by then, and I'd come back to my small town so that he and I could watch the eclipse together.

Of course, when it actually arrived, no one traveled here because they thought the light pollution was too great. And of course, I was not a radio astronomer, but a bus driver at the end of my route, soon to hand the keys over to a self-driving machine.

And of course, we did not watch it together, because at the time of the eclipse, he had been gone a full decade, which I realize now is precisely about the time the stars went out.

He wrote the date of the eclipse on a star chart that lived on my ceiling in our two-bedroom apartment on Main Street, and at night I would look at the date and imagine how different my life would be when that day came, when everything aligned in the town I grew up in. I imagined that date over the years, as it grew closer, and I imagined all the ways we thought the world would be when that date came, then watched and listened as those expectations unraveled.

At the exact moment of totality my déjà vu was so intense I had to sit on the ground and breathe slowly. It was so intense—I'm ashamed to admit this—at the exact moment of totality, I had to look away.

133

I study now in any moment I have free time, on the walk to my shifts driving the bus, as I'm grocery shopping, in the shower, as I'm eating all my meals. Instead of reading them stories, I recite laws and principles and equations to the triplets at night as they fall asleep.

But there is something else I have been spending my time thinking about, the mystery propelling my bus forward, the mystery that lines my routes.

"Who made the nests?" I ask Sulien.

And then I ask Uri and Luce. "Who made the nests?"

No one has any leads, no ideas. But when I ask them, they give me looks like I myself should know.

"Who made the nests?" I ask the NO people and the YES people at The Demonstration, but they only shake their heads in a direction corresponding with their side.

"Who made the nests?" I ask the triplets, whisper into the crowns of their heads as I am lifting them into or out of their bed.

And then, to my surprise, One of the Triplets responds.

"The ghost of birds," One of the Triplets says, and the other two look at me blinking as though the question was absurd.

132

The globes in Luce's yard—the yard that used to be the yard of my father and his fathers before him—are flawed. Each globe has something wrong with it. They are globes that my grandfathers almost discarded but chose to plant, and in planting, formed a garden of fictional Earths. For some, the orb is misshapen, while others are covered in misprinted strips of map. Still others were mishandled, the sphere smashed in somewhere, or weren't crafted correctly, the angle not quite at 23.5 degrees. Whatever their ailment or mistake, all of them are too damaged to have been salvaged and too spoiled to have been revised. My grandfathers started planting them one at a time in the front yard, perched on tall poles or mounted low to the ground, until the yard began to fill. Sometimes I sit on Luce's porch and imagine the years unfolding, thirty years in a minute, watch the yard get populated and fill in with globes. Globes dotting the landscape then peppering it, globes filling it up completely, at every height and of every conceivable size. I know that yard of globes like I know the stars in the sky, and I know from Luce the exact order every globe appeared. Now, all these years later, the collection is exquisite, and we have had to craft a dirt path winding through the yard so that we can visit each one.

I'm filling Luce in on the new nest while she weaves brand-new laces into her steel-toed boots. I can see that something's bothering her, so I ask her about the new job.

"How're things at The Farm? Since the promotion?" I ask her, and she shakes her head back and forth. This is it, I can tell—the source of her concern.

But Luce, of course, is Luce, and she won't tell me. She just keeps shaking her head and breathing heavily.

Then she changes the subject. "How is Uri taking to his wings?"

I watch her thread her boots. "He loves them. Tucks in postcards and flowers, rocks and photographs. They are already getting quite full."

She nods to herself. "In a way, the nests are a kind of theater, too," she says. Then she says: "*Theater*. Late middle English. From Old French and Greek *theatron*. Meaning 'to behold.'"

I look at the globes in the front yard, let my eyes follow the tangential dirt path that leads a person on a tour to visit each of them.

"You really consider the nests theater?" I ask her.

"Sure," she says. "They're fictional. They're on display. They are there for others 'to behold,'" she says. "But then, all of life is theater, when you boil it right down."

"You mean how everyone changes depending on who they're around?"

"Sure. And also this notion your father used to have, that I've been thinking about lately. This notion about what all this is. What it means," she says, and she waves absently all around her.

"What notion?"

Luce takes in a deep breath, then lets it out very loudly. She pulls the two ends of the laces up and they aren't the same length, so she begins to undo her work. "Don't think you want to hear," she says.

"No, I do," I say. A soft breeze makes some of the globes turn. "I want to hear this notion. This notion of my father's."

"Okay," she says. "All right."

What she says then is this: toward the end, my father conveyed to Luce that he had come to a kind of understanding that the world was not what it appeared to be. He came to believe that what we see as reality—what we recognize as the world around us—is actually a kind of imitation world, a false set, like on a stage. He thought that something on some other plane, in some other dimension, had placed us here to navigate this fiction so that they could see and hear and witness—"so that they might behold"—what it is we choose to do. He thought—and Luce does not hesitate to tell me this—he thought that everything around us was artificial, despite us being real.

I cannot tell what it is that she's describing—if this is something spiritual or psychological, or even a kind of allegory to be taken sincerely, but not literally. It seems, as she keeps talking, that it is all of these and more. She is telling me that this is one of the notions that came to be a way he shaped his life.

"How long did he think this way?" I ask her.

"For a while," she says. "For a long time. Since before you were born."

"Why didn't he tell me?"

"Because I told him not to," she says, threading the laces through the eyes of her shoes.

"He's been gone over a decade. Why is this coming up now?"

"Remembered after the eclipse," she says, but I can tell she's not telling me everything. There is a look in her eyes that feels like she's hiding something. "Truth is, he and I used to think about the day of the eclipse since we were kids. Knew our town was in the path of totality."

I think of the star chart in my bedroom, the date he'd written in the corner, wonder how long he'd actually been anchored to that date.

Then Luce says, "When we were little, before we knew anything, we used to imagine the world was something like that. Something unreal. It was a childhood fantasy that he held on to."

I look out over the field of flawed globes and wonder how much of that yard influenced what she is telling me now.

Luce pulls up the laces again and they are even and she puts that boot aside and starts in on the other one.

"Sounds to me like a kind of theology," I say.

"He said it was more like a theory," she tells me. "*Theory,*" she says, "from the Greek *theōros,* meaning 'spectator.'"

"Just like *theatron,*" I say then, and I gently mimic her voice when I say: "*Theater.* From Greek *theatron.* Meaning 'to behold.'"

"Uri says that the stage is the whole of the world," she says. "But what interested your father is what unfolds when things happen off-stage. Like right now. You and me, we're here," she says. "How do we know that the triplets are in their room right now, that there are triplets at all?"

I reach for the baby monitor but I realize suddenly we're not at my duplex. We're at her house, and it is Uri's night.

"'Don't you think it's funny,' he would say, 'that in a world that relies so much on circles and cycles and orbits, time is a line?'"

I clear my throat and rearrange my legs.

"He truly, absolutely believed that some other force was in charge," she says, and she pulls the laces of the second shoe up to discover they are perfectly even. "Toward the end he would tell me all the time: Something else is structuring what and how we know—where we look and when we see. Why we come to understand things. Why we don't."

"And you believed him? I mean, Luce. Some of the things he said to us. To me. The things he'd say to me." I look at her, shake my head.

"I didn't believe him, no. But I tried to understand him. Tried to listen. Felt wrong not to try."

I am quiet for a minute, because I, too, am trying to do a better job of listening, of understanding, even that which escapes the span of my belief. If my déjà vu has taught me nothing else, it has taught me this: we do not have access to all the secrets the universe keeps.

"Something else is structuring what and how we know," I repeat, trying out the idea in my mouth and in my mind. "Seems less like the question is who," I say, "and more like the question is why."

"Same reason we watch theater," she says. "To witness someone else display the ways humans behave because we aren't able or willing to see it ourselves."

"Guess if he was right, if some other consciousness is governing all this, then all our drama—on stage and off—is all for entertainment."

"There is another possibility," Luce says, taking off her backup boots and putting on her newly-laced ones. "Perhaps we're playing out some kind of pattern that may be useful to be observed. What happens when this kind of problem surfaces, or that kind of conundrum unfolds. In what ways do people come together and in what ways do people fall apart."

"That seems cruel," I say, and just as I'm starting to get angry, recognizing and reflecting on my father's sorrow, I realize the other side of it. "That also seems smart."

"Think about it like Uri would," Luce says, picking at the fraying hem of her pants. "A play doesn't start with each of the characters' birth. It starts wherever it needs to start for the playwright to do the work that needs to be done. And just as the beginning is determined, there is also always an end. And when this experiment ends, your father thought, all that will be left is a recording, a trace, like your tape and videocassettes. All that will be left is whatever can be learned by the something or someone larger than us out there in the ether. The something or someone seeing themselves played out in the things that we do. Familiar but also estranged."

"Luce, please. It sounds like you believe him."

She shakes her head hard from side to side. "Not what I'm saying. Just been thinking a lot about some of what he said. Since the eclipse. Trying to listen to him, the echoes of him."

I don't know what to say, so I say nothing. I look out over the yard of my grandfathers, the yard that now belongs to Luce.

"But then, you would know better than me," she says, tying the laces of her boots.

"Why do you say that?" I say, and for a moment I think she is telling me that I would know because I am my father's daughter.

But that's not what she means. I can tell because she looks up with her eyebrows raised.

"You're talking about space," I say. "You're saying some other lifeform is responsible for building this world and everyone in it."

She shrugs and grunts once. "Truth is, I wonder if it offers the smallest bit of comfort."

"Knowing our whole reality is some technosignature from a higher consciousness?" I ask.

She snorts, smiles. "What the hell is a technosignature?"

"It's the evidence of advanced cognizance out there detectible because of their data's pollution," I say.

"You're sharper than you give yourself credit for," she says, and then, "No, it's not knowing we're living in a reproduction world that gives comfort. I think it's knowing we don't know and never will. That's what we talked about when we were little—knowing that if all of this was an imitation crafted by something else, that we'd never know who or why. Theory and theater share an etymology. It's all just speculation, spectating. It's all spectral," she says, and stands up, wiggles her feet a bit to see how the laces feel.

She looks at me. My stomach is turning—my body is pulsing, but I can't tell if it is pulsing with dread or with awe.

"I said it. I told you. Said you wouldn't want to hear." She stomps a few times, jogs up and down the three stairs of the porch. Then she spins the nearest globe with her hand, and I watch it turn fast, then more slowly.

The globe stops spinning and she says very softly, "He would never tell you *what* to think. He would not do that. He always felt you alone decide what it is you believe. What he liked to do was give you something to think *about*."

And then she says something that makes my heart hurt.

"I wish you could have seen him when he was well. I mean, really well. Before you were born. When he was well, he was something else, your father." She says, "I miss him every day."

I will pass the test, I think then. There is no other conclusion. And then I embrace Luce around her center and hold her and she lets me because she knows that this is the only way I give a hug.

131

SULIEN: I'm worried about her.

URI: Me, too.

SULIEN: What can we do?

URI: Be patient. And maybe dust off your old recipe for cinnamon nutmeg chocolate chip cookies. She's going to need comfort food.

130

Once, before my father died, The Only Person I've Ever Loved had chosen a globe in this front yard and spun it. "I'm going to stop it in a random place, and that's where we're going to live. You and me. In the future."

She waited a minute, hummed a song I did not recognize. Then she took her finger and touched the globe and it stopped spinning instantly.

But when we looked at the place where she pointed, we discovered her finger had landed precisely on the point that marked our town.

129

On my route that next morning, as I drive by the homes of the citizens of this small town, the YES people and the NO people, not a single soul on my bus, no one in transit at all at least in the analog world, me going in circles alone, something strikes me: every nest that has been erected is visible on my route. It is as though the builder of the nests placed them strategically where Route 0 travels to ensure that every person who entered that bus would witness the homes of these lost species. The problem being that I drive a zombie route.

When I get home, I follow the sounds of Luce reading and open the door to the triplets' room. They are huddled around her feet, lying down and looking up while she sits in the rocking chair, manuscript open. Luce doesn't notice me enter the room, but the triplets do, and they each give me a smile. Luce keeps reading, and I recognize this monologue as a pivotal moment in Act 3. Then the triplets giggle and Luce sees me in the doorway, starts. She looks just like my father.

"Uri's got another ending. He's having me run it by the triplets."

I look at the triplets curled around Luce's feet. "What do you think?" I ask them, and all three give me a hesitant nod.

"You want to listen? Only a few pages left," Luce says, her thumb flipping through the manuscript.

"Something tells me this won't be his last ending," I tell her, and she grunts a laugh.

I wave to the triplets and shut the door, lean my back against it. I listen to Luce's voice reading Uri's manuscript on the other side.

I look up then and am surprised to see the entrance to the attic. It's amazing what we forget until something out of the ordinary— some shift in our routine or change in our schedule—forces us to face it. My side of the duplex has an attic, of course, the attic where I have not been in a very long time. I reach up and pull on the string that lets the ladder down, and then I go up. It isn't large here—just enough room for a few boxes. I pull an unmarked one down.

In the hallway, on the ground, I open the box and there, right on top, is what I'm looking for: my old handheld two-way radio.

Through the door, I hear Luce's voice rise and then fall, and the triplets take in a deep and audible breath, the sound of disbelief.

I had only been given one side of the two-way radio. The other, my father told me, lived on another plane. When I was lonely, I needed only to turn this on and someone else, someone far away in another world, would respond to me, if I was lonely enough. If not, no one would respond, and I would know that the loneliness I thought I was feeling was not loneliness at all but something else: boredom or nostalgia.

Now I wonder if what he told me was related to his ideas about our world being an imitation.

I set the two-way radio on the ground and close the box back up, replace it in the attic where I'd put it years ago, when Uri and I had moved into the duplex. I fold the stairs up and use the string to very carefully and quietly guide the attic door shut.

Then I walk across the hall to my window and turn the radio on. To my amazement, the batteries still work and the sound of static emerges. I lean out my window and turn the dial to a different frequency and the white noise shifts in tone.

I press the button while I whisper into the handheld machine, "Are you there?"

I don't know who "you" is. It's a general kind of gesture.

"Are you there?" I say into the mouthpiece and then I listen for a response.

I wait for a while, my body half out the window, every now and again asking if anyone is there. And then the static shifts a bit, then quiets, and amplifies again, quiets one more time.

And then—then. I hear a sound. Then—my god—I hear a sound and the sound—I must be hearing wrong, not listening closely enough.

I hang outside the window and press my ear to the pores of the microphone piece and what I hear can't be what I think.

It sounds like a human breathing.

128

THE GHOST OF BIRDS: *[Indecipherable.]*

127

There are ten days before I take the test, and I am doing everything in my core, everything in my body to keep the knowledge in. I sleep and eat and sing and drive and breathe relativity and isotopes and the Boltzmann constant and the Norton equivalent. At The Demonstration, I yell NO or YES depending on which side I am in support of that day, but in my mind it is harmonic oscillators and the Doppler effect, Faraday's law of induction. I am ten days away and I am pure math—I am invincible in my belief. There is nothing but radio astronomy before me, about me, running through me. It's like a fog, the way it hangs, goes into my head and exits my mouth and ears, every pore of my skin. I am all and only radio astronomy, such that I sometimes forget I have a body at all. I look around at the world and while I see its concreteness, I also see the principles and laws and equations secretly governing that concreteness, see through the illusion and toward the invisible structures that manage the real.

I am all and only radio astronomy, and if all I am is what I know—like Luce says, we are just words—then when I take this test, what I need to do is put myself there, lay myself before the test and offer it myself. There is nothing in me but radio astronomy, and I realize that this is not something I feel.

It is like the once-forthcoming-now-past eclipse, mathematically proven right down to the date and time decades in advance.

I am all and only radio astronomy, and it is not something that I feel. It is something that I know.

126

A week before the eclipse, the triplets and I went to the playground before Uri delivered our dinner. I pushed them on the swings, helped them mount the stairs to use the slide, held each of them up while they pretended they were conquering the monkey bars. I spun them on the merry-go-round, the chipped paint on the metal parts coming off onto my palms.

They spent a lot of time on the merry-go-round. They wanted to spin faster and faster. They said they could feel it slowing and that I had to keep it going at the same pace. It made me think of the globes, but also, as I kept spinning them, as they kept gently insisting I was letting it slow too much, I got to thinking about how we are spinning, too, on Earth's surface, a spinning we can't feel.

Then, suddenly, I realized this was dangerous. Shit, I thought, I shouldn't have let them get me to spin it this fast.

I stopped then, pulling the handlebars in the opposite direction, using my feet planted in the ground to halt the flat plane on which the triplets were sitting. I was sweating, my hands raw from the metal bars. They didn't object when I stopped.

When they got off, I remember very specifically that they did not lose their balance—they stepped down and the three of them gathered together, walking in a perfect line, not a bit unstable after all that turning.

Then the triplets—all three of them—they grabbed each other's hands and One of them told me that a black hole was coming. "I'm sorry?" I asked, and Another said, "There is a black hole and it is coming for us." I shook my head and corrected them: "An eclipse, you mean. There's no black hole. You mean the eclipse." And I crouched down to their level and smiled, but they looked at me with wide eyes and blank faces and shook their heads. "A black hole," the Third said, and I looked into the eyes of the three beings that I harvested inside my body and I wondered what was behind those eyes, those eyes that themselves were eclipsing something I could not then and have not since quite found.

The world was spinning but I couldn't feel it.

I stood up and breathed deeply. A black hole, I thought then, is coming.

In this way, briefly, I let myself believe.

125

The Two-Way Radio: *[Static.]*

124

There are five days until I take the test. Luce has forced me downstairs for a cigarette, and then she forces me on a walk and I recite to her everything I have covered in the last few days in preparation for the test. I am lecturing and pointing out historical context to developments in theories and distinctions between principles and defining concepts and comparing and contrasting laws with other laws. Eventually we wind up at her house and sit down on her porch, and she says that we can talk about anything—anything—other than astronomy.

The problem that seems most before me is the test, but I think then about the other problem lingering on the periphery of my life.

"How did you know?" I ask, looking out over my grandfathers' labyrinth of globes.

"Know what?" Luce says.

"How did you know you were NO?"

Luce rolls her shoulders. A breeze comes in. A few of the globes start spinning. "You reflect on it for a long time. You weigh the pros and cons. You consider what you care about, where you want to center your life, how that philosophy will shape everything that comes thereafter."

"But I've done all that. Been doing it for years. I just can't come to the right conclusion," I tell her. "I feel like—"

"Stop," she says, interrupting me. "Stop saying what you feel. Tell me what you know," she says.

I sit there for a very long time and try to summon what it is that I know, but all I get is radio astronomy. I get nothing about myself. "I don't work that way," I tell her. "When it comes to who I am, you know I go by feel." She sighs, and I can tell I've disappointed her.

"That's exactly what I thought you would say," she says. "And it's going to doom you."

Then Luce grabs my neck with the angle of her arm and pulls my head into her chest, which is one of three ways that Luce gives a hug.

She smells like cigarettes and sweat and the paste that my grandfathers used to make the globes and a bit, just the tiniest bit, a whiff, I would say—like my father.

123

There are three days until I take the test, and I am all heat and wind and celestial energy. I am only time denoted by the speed of light.

Every month, on a night I have the triplets, Uri and Luce meet up to visit the graveyard. It turns out their siblings aren't buried too far from each other, so they bring flowers in the spring or tools to clean up the weeds in the late summer or grave blankets in the winter months. I used to go with them and we'd take the triplets along, but we learned quickly that graveyards make all three of them behave strangely.

This Tuesday Luce and Uri asked me if I wanted them to skip so they could watch the triplets while I studied. But the test is now hours away, and I am all radio astronomy. Nothing can touch me or the fact of me passing this test. Everything in me is already there. It's now all just getting it out.

They are gone a long while, and it's only after night has set in that they return. I am in the triplets' room looking out the window when I see them coming down the dirt path next to the street, the place where—if this town were a different town—there would be a sidewalk.

They are the two people I care for most in the world, besides the triplets, and they are walking shoulder to shoulder and talking so comfortably I grow envious. Uri laughs and nods to Luce while she speaks, then Uri responds and Luce gives a light howl and a knee slap. Uri pushes her gently but she almost loses her balance and she says something loud and they both fall into laughter.

When they part at our driveway, I come onto the porch and meet Uri there with a beer.

"What do you talk about?" I ask him.

"Oh," Uri says, and takes a big swig. "Our siblings. Just old stories about our siblings," he says. "What it means to have had siblings and lost them."

For a minute I want to ask him more, but then I realize this is private, something children without siblings like myself can't understand.

The test is three days away. I think of the law of threes in storytelling which is a rule, a principle, but it has nothing to do with physics. And I think of the triplets in their room. They have something I don't have, and I hope they find a way to be together all their long and complex lives. No matter if those lives are without birds. No matter if those lives are without stars.

The world is big and life is short and I will pass this test. And the triplets will stay together and grow and change, even as—especially as—the world around them changes, too. Because soon, very soon, The Crisis will become something else. It will tip one way or the other, and whichever direction it goes, it's going to mean something new.

They could live beyond the end of this millennium, I think. And then I think of my own future, my life transposed over the life of a radio astronomer. I sit on our porch and listen to Uri recite the lines of his play while I imagine the future a millennium from now, what kind of world it will be.

122

"Why do you think," I once asked The Only Person I've Ever Loved, "that Girl in Glass Vessel is just about a girl? Aren't all people sort of in their own glass vessels?"

And she said, "We're all in vessels. But a young woman suffering is the oldest tale people tell. You know?"

She was biting her nails. I very slowly, very gently pulled her hand away from her mouth.

She looked out the window. "What I've always found disturbing about Girl in Glass Vessel is that as soon as she's free to face reality—as soon as she leaves behind all the layers of artificiality she was born into—that is the same moment in which she disappears."

121

Theater, Uri says, can never mean the same thing for each member of the audience, because—while they may see the same scripted action—each member witnesses a different drama.

120

There are forty hours until the test, and I am kinetic. I am all potential.

"How is life at The Farm since the promotion?" I ask Luce after she's spent a good week or so changing the subject when I bring it up.

Luce looks at the ground.

"Truthfully?" she says. "It's complicated. But it's not the promotion. Working at The Farm has been complicated since the start. When it was The Factory, I understood things, knew what we were producing. I understood the work we were taking on. It was work that I was born into, work my fathers did and their fathers before them. There was a concrete product and we made it, then we assembled it, then we shipped it along. But at The Farm—well, it's different. I'm running cable every day, keeping the coolant in the warehouse, managing the servers. But I don't know what precisely is happening in those cables. I'm not sure what I'm letting unfold, what I am responsible for making happen. It's all invisible, covert. I mean, think of all the everything that happens on the internet. Over the internet. In? Is the internet a place you get inside or a place you transpose yourself over or a place you witness from afar?"

I think of the science of optics, how light travels more slowly in water, and I shrug.

"Think of all that unfolds there, and I'm the one making that data get from one part of the world to the next, from one human palm to another," she says. "I don't know. Maybe it's just the shift from production to service, but I get uncomfortable not knowing how the work that I do translates to the world outside The Farm." She looks up at the duplex and I follow her gaze and there is Uri in the window, mouthing the words to his play.

"But, hell," she says, "I've got a job. It's not right to complain about it in front of you when yours is just about gone."

"Complain away. I've done enough of that to you between the routes and the triplets," I tell her. I will pass this test. This test will be passed, I tell myself.

"It's just that I use my hands," she says. "I've always used my hands to make things. Now I don't know what my hands are doing." She opens her palms and looks at them then like they will give her the answer.

I slap her palms with mine and hold her hands. "Why don't you try making a globe?"

She scoffs, turns away. "I told you. I don't have it in me to make something round. All I know is lines. Production lines, now lines of cable, lines of communication, since The Factory became The Farm. Wouldn't know where to start with making something into a kind of circle."

"But Luce, you made Uri's wings. How did you do that?" I ask her.

She is silent. We can hear Uri reciting the lines of the play through his cracked window, his voice rising resolutely.

"You took a piece of wire and you bent it. Where you start," I say, stealing her cigarette, "is taking the line and giving it an arc."

Exponents and parabolas, I think. The test will be passed. I take a deep drag of the cigarette. The future is the test being passed. The future is tomorrow, the future is both YES and NO, I think. And then I think of the moment in 4.5 billion years when the Milky Way collides with Andromeda.

119

There are twenty-four hours until the test, and as far as I'm concerned, the test is over, I have passed, and I am already at a desk working on the sky.

When I was young, star charts filled the walls of my room. My father was the present, and those charts became my future. I was less than a decade old, and I would feel the full weight of that decade in my bones, in the way the heft of my head would dent the pillow, in the way night after night I'd sleep so deeply that in the morning, I'd be distraught that I had to be awake.

I would cross my arms behind my head and instead of crying—for that, I had learned early, was no use to anyone—instead of crying, I would repeat the day of the eclipse over and over, thinking how much different—how much better—my life would be then.

There are twenty-four hours until the test, and the world around me feels like it is spinning and I am gliding through time, spectral, like the wind carries a seed. There are twenty-four hours until the test, and I almost want to skip them, speed up life like on the VCR and get there now so I can begin to become what I know that I already am.

118

"It's funny," The Only Person I've Ever Loved said once, "you want to be a radio astronomer. I want to be an architect." We were smoking candy cigarettes, which we had taken up to try to help her stop biting her fingernails.

"What's funny about that?" I asked, pulling another one from the carton since she'd just eaten the one she'd been smoking.

"The meaning is different, of course, but—I can't believe I just realized this—we both want to work with space."

117

ONE OF THE TRIPLETS: Could we hear the story of the Girl in Glass Vessel tonight?

HER: We're putting that story on hold for a while.

ANOTHER OF THE TRIPLETS: Please! Girl in Glass Vessel!

HER: A solid effort, my friends, but no. How about Chicken Little?

THE THIRD OF THE TRIPLETS: I like the planetarium best. The way the girl is locked inside it.

HER: Yes. But! No Girl in Glass Vessel tonight.

ONE OF THE TRIPLETS: And the ghost of birds. Telling the story. From outside the planetarium.

HER: Chicken Little it is.

ANOTHER OF THE TRIPLETS: I want to be a girl in a glass vessel.

HER: [*Beat.*] What?

ANOTHER OF THE TRIPLETS: I want to be a girl in a glass vessel!

THE THIRD OF THE TRIPLETS: Yes! Me, too. Me, too.

ONE OF THE TRIPLETS: And me!

[*The triplets mime that they are pressing invisible shells around them.*]

HER: Nope. No, no—all right now—stop. You do not want to be the protagonist of that story.

ONE OF THE TRIPLETS: Then I want to be Chicken Little.

HER: You also—trust me on this—you also do not want to be her.

ANOTHER OF THE TRIPLETS: I don't want to be Chicken Little or the Girl in Glass Vessel. I want to be in both stories.

ONE OF THE TRIPLETS: You can't be in both stories.

ANOTHER OF THE TRIPLETS: Yes, I can.

THE THIRD OF THE TRIPLETS: How?

ANOTHER OF THE TRIPLETS: I want to be the sky.

116

There are eighteen hours until the test when it happens.

The day is a cool one, and I've opened all the windows, a beautiful breeze coursing through the bus.

As I make the turn, I see a passenger there at the Fourth and Federal bus stop. It's a person with one hand on their hip and the other over their eye, shielding it from the sun's haze. The person is dressed in many layers of black that look, interchangeably, like a dress, a cloak, a suit, a cape, and pajamas all at once. It is a conundrum of an outfit, but then, as I pull up and open the doors, when I see the form of the passenger, I know why it seems that way. I can feel the blood pulsing inside me, moving straight to my face.

There, standing at the stop, is The Only Person I've Ever Loved.

I pull the lever that opens the bus doors and she steps onto the bus. She starts to put her bills into the machine that collects the bus fare but I hold my hand over the opening, tell her this ride's on me.

She slips into a seat toward the middle of the bus, scoots all the way to the window.

"Where are you headed?" I ask her.

"Where's this route go?" she responds.

"In circles," I say, and close the doors and look behind me for traffic. Then I merge.

"It's good to see you," she says. "I tried to make it back for the eclipse, but life outside this town moves quickly. First it was a year ago, then yesterday. I lost track of time," she says, looking out the window.

"Don't be so sure you lost track of time. It could have lost track of you. Time moves differently outside of this town," I say, though the truth is I would not know, since I have never left.

"You look well," she says, and for a minute, I wonder if she knows, if somehow she found out that she is The Only Person I've Ever Loved. But that is impossible, I think, making a left on Division Street. I only found out myself after she'd gone.

"You're right about time moving differently here. I was just talking to Sulien about that. This town is governed by an invisible system," she says, and she folds her arms and puts them over the seatback in front of her. She tilts her head. "And the system is solar."

"You spoke with Sulien?" She nods her head once, and I try not to be hurt. I breathe in and out for a moment, slow before a four-way stop. Look both ways. "What do you mean, solar?" I say. "You mean the eclipse?"

"No, no. Or yes—yes, I mean the eclipse, but also that old town legend," she says. And her answer makes me wonder what might have happened if she'd stayed through her young adulthood, whether she'd be a YES or NO person. Whether I would be a YES or NO person based on her decision, and not caught in this limbo, this strange space between.

"Well, what are you doing in town if you missed the eclipse?"

"Just thought I'd stick around a while. Heard about the nests," she says. "It's strange," she says, too loudly, "this route. You can see all of them." She gestures out the window, but her eyes stayed locked on the rearview mirror.

I want to say, how would you know? You don't know this route and you've left this town. But I don't want to fuel the tension hovering heavy in the air.

"Is there somewhere specific I can drop you?" I ask, trying to get the thought out of my head.

"You can drop me off outside of the town limits," she says.

"This route doesn't go that way," I tell her.

"You could change up the route," she tells me. "You could leave." Then she says a bit louder: "You could leave, you know. Right now. You could come with me."

There is a long silence before she says what she says next.

"Come with me." Her voice is low and bold, and I realize then she hasn't changed a bit. "Leave here and go anywhere else. Leave with me."

"You know all those years of listening has left me struggling to hear," I tell her. "Please speak up."

"You heard me," she says. "You can get out of here. Today." She clears her throat and then says more softly. "There are still places left where you can see the stars."

And there it is and she knows it—she's hit my soft part, the tenderest portion of me. I can feel the blood orbiting my body; I can feel it heat up. It is a feeling like a hot bath on a cold night, but one that starts inside you and then works its way out to your flesh instead of the other way around.

"You know that's impossible," I tell her, "because it's too late," I say, "because the triplets."

"You don't owe them anything. It was a transaction that didn't go as planned."

I pull the bus over and put it in park, turn on the emergency lights. I turn around and look at her directly.

"You—"

I want to tell her, I almost say it—I am a breath away from calling her The Only Person I've Ever Loved.

"You!" I say instead. "You left! You! Left! I only took the surrogate gig in the first place because you left," I tell her. "We were supposed to get out together. We weren't supposed to be a cliché. Why didn't you take me with you?"

She bites her nails then, just like she always used to—I guess some roles don't change, no matter on what stage they are performed—and she says: "When you're faced with the chance to escape, you take it. You don't spend time packing a bag and waiting around for someone else."

We happen to be parked in front of the bald eagle nest. We both look out the window.

"You'd get it if you were able to leave this place. I'm giving you that chance now. Leave with me," she says. "Maybe everything that has happened has happened so that in this moment you can leave.

Everything has been pointing toward right now."

Cause and effect, I think. But then I think of my grandfathers' globes and the way the past isn't removed, it's just eclipsed. "Three humans," I say to her, adjusting my sweater vest and tie, "were incubated inside of my body and when the time came for them to escape, the parents I thought I was handing them to—really brilliant, beautiful people, actually wonderful people—they'd been killed. You know me better than anyone else. I could never leave now."

She sits back in the seat. "You're right." She bites her nails, spitting out what she uses her teeth to pull from her fingers. "You're right," and the way she says it is like she's just realized it herself. Then she says: "I tried. I get points for trying," and she smooths out the layers of fabric that hug her form.

"You do not get points. Because there are no points. Because this isn't a game," I tell her, and I mean it. This isn't a game at all. No one is going to win, not the YES people and not the NO people. The debate will rage on forever.

I get in my seat and buckle up and then we drive a bit longer and I get to thinking about love. I get to thinking about suturing your life to someone else, about the risk in that, the possible joy, the way the risk is bound up with the joy. I think for a moment that I should tell her—I should tell her she is The Only Person I've Ever Loved. But something tells me that she probably already knows. She probably knew before I knew and she probably never loved me back. Love, I think then, must be like the white of an egg wrapped around a yolk made of grief. Then I remember there aren't birds anymore.

"What did you mean by the old legend about this town being governed by a system?" I ask her.

"The legend. You know the town legend," she says.

"No."

"That this town is all there is. That over this town was laid a solar system, and beyond this town there is nothing but the rest of the vast and empty universe."

I sigh then, very loudly. "The rest of the universe is the opposite of empty," I tell her. "There are over two trillion galaxies that we have identified—that we've *identified*. There are four hundred billion exoplanets in the Milky Way *alone*. Beyond our solar system, space is full."

"It's just a legend. It's not real," she says. "Plus, I've left this town. I promise you there's more beyond it."

I ignore her. "Galaxies," I'm saying, looking both ways and making a right on Federal, rounding back the way we came, "not just planetary systems. And the number of stars—it's practically infinite. There are whole rings of planets we're just now finding out about," I hear myself saying, and then when I hear myself say the word *rings* I am stung with another: Saturn.

Saturn, just beyond the road that leads nowhere.

I breathe very slowly and hear her say again that it's just a legend, but that she loves hearing me talk about space, my passion for space, and isn't it funny that we both work with space, and what do I think of the nests? she asks me, staring hard into the rearview mirror. What do I think of the nests? she asks, and I am breathing slowly and stopping at a four-way and looking both directions twice. The nests, she says, and I think, the system, but she says, the nests, the nests, and I am elsewhere for I do not know how long, and then I hear the bell that signals a stop has been requested.

As I'm making my way to the Fourth and Federal stop, she moves to a seat at the front and leans in close. "You say this route goes in circles," she says. "Have you ever gone the opposite direction?"

"What do you mean." It comes out sounding more tired than I'd intended.

"Have you ever gone the opposite way. Turned the bus around," she says, and we're in front of her stop, the place where I picked her up. She has gone, essentially, nowhere.

"What are you saying?" I ask as I'm putting the bus in park.

She stands up. "Turn the bus around. Might mean you get to see the same world through a new lens," she says, and she grabs my chin with her hand and gets really close to my face, sinks her gaze into me, and I think for a moment she is going to shake my head, either YES or NO. She is going to give me some insight into myself. Tell me about myself, I want to ask her, tell me what I've never been able to learn about myself on my own. But I don't say that and she doesn't shake my head at all. Instead, she kisses the top of my head very quickly and briefly—so briefly—as she cups my cheek.

"Go the opposite direction," she tells me, and hops off the bus.

There goes the Only Person I've Ever Loved.

She may never return.

I close the bus doors then and merge back into traffic. I realize she never apologized and now, I assume, she never will.

There are seventeen hours until the test. I stay the course, keep going the route I've been prescribed, the route I'll continue following until the bus drives itself.

115

Girl in Glass Vessel goes like this.

There's a girl and she's in a glass vessel. It's tight in there. Sometimes the glass stretches and the orb gives her some room and she can walk around a bit, and sometimes the vessel gets really snug around her body, like an egg. The glass vessel constricts and expands based on the tension in the world outside it and the tension of the world inside the girl. The girl and her glass vessel exist inside a planetarium, so she can't see the real night sky. She tells her story alone in her transparent world, thinking she is in charge of what is heard, but the whole story is curated and governed by the ghost of birds.

The girl in the glass vessel wants desperately to get out of the glass vessel, and she shares this desire with the planetarium who wishes it was the real night sky. They want to be real and free of the constrictions their institutions have imposed on them. This is a problem, the ghost of birds conveys to the listener, though covertly, and that problem is ongoing and sincere. The girl in the glass vessel and the planetarium are bound together in this, their shared challenge.

Until one day the planetarium splits itself open. It folds itself open, spread like a book, and finally it is exposed to the real night sky. The planetarium is thrilled, the ghost of birds makes clear, and when the planetarium asks what the girl in the glass vessel thinks, she nods and smiles and weeps inside her orb. Suddenly, it starts raining, and the rain causes the glass to dissolve around the girl, because until this point the planetarium had protected her from precipitation. For a moment, as she watches the glass around her dissolve, she cannot breathe because she is so moved by the world outside of her glass shell. She has never faced any kind of weather, has never experienced the stark and stunning truth of the real atmosphere around her, the galaxy above. For a moment—briefly— she is facing the world outside of the vessel, before she realizes that she cannot breathe. It is first a product of awe but shortly thereafter she cannot breathe for another reason—it becomes clear to her in one final, poignant moment that the glass vessel protected her from the elements outside, elements that are now breaking her down and apart. Slowly, she stops being alive and the rain, like the glass vessel, dissolves her, too.

Then there is only the planetarium. The planetarium quickly becomes aware of its own artifice when it sees the brilliance of the real night sky. It realizes its whole life has been bound to imitation, but the true sorrow is that it cannot return to even that, since it has ruined itself in the process of trying to see what is real. While it takes the planetarium much longer than the girl—it takes years and years, centuries, millennia—it, too, lies in ruins until it dissolves. This is how the planetarium comes to understand grief.

The ghost of birds conveys then that if one visits this site now, one would note that there is nothing left, and as such, this site could be anywhere—your park or library, your market or backyard, the place where you are sitting. Where once was the grief that comes with exposure, now there is nothing but the ghost of birds telling you this tale. The place where the story ends leads to the story's own beginning—the story is conveyed on a loop—so if you are told the story of Girl in Glass Vessel even once, you are locked in, bound to the tale forever. If you hear it even once, then it will keep repeating, over and over again inside your ear, until you learn not to listen. All children are told this tale, and as they grow older and into adulthood, their ability to listen fades. But if you are an adult and if you choose to listen carefully, if you choose to truly hear, then what you will find under the sound of the rest of your adult life is this: the ghost of birds whispering into your ear the story of the girl in the glass vessel. Forever and always, and even after that.

114

THE SERVER FARM: *[A soft hum.]*

113

Sometimes at night when I'm lying in bed, I recall the moment just after totality. There was totality and then, for those who watched—I couldn't—the sun peeked back out from behind the moon and it wasn't dark anymore and the earth kept spinning and life kept moving in a direction that felt like forward.

But something strange happens when I reach the precipice of sleep. Like a dream I can't control, my brain switches to another version of what happened, to a fictional future that didn't unfold. Instead of the moon moving across the sun, waning now instead of waxing, the sun and the moon don't move. The moon stays there and time is passing but nothing is happening. And then the dark that covers the sun grows larger, is actually growing toward us, expanding out. And I look over at Uri and Sulien and Luce and the YES people and the NO people, I look over at the triplets, and I see that they are—all of them—their bodies are stretching. They are stretching and the trees are stretching and the field is stretching and it is beautiful, the way the world expands and smears itself across itself, and I look at my own body and I am stretching, too.

I think then of the etymology of *intent*—to expand.

Beyond the black hole is the white hole, where time reverses and no one—not one single human—has ever been there, but I know in my bones that I'm about to be. I'm about to enter the event horizon, and understand what happens on the other side of time.

The Crisis is over and things have tipped the wrong way. The Crisis is over and what I think then is the order is wrong, always has been. First it is the end and then the middle. It's only after that— only after the end and the middle when everything begins.

112

The day of the test is a cold one. I wear a button-up shirt under an oversized sweater and then pull on my overalls.

Everything around me is light and air and the world speeds up like on a VCR—I walk out of my bedroom door and the triplets are up and running around downstairs playing tag and Uri is making me breakfast full of protein, he says, which helps you to think, and Luce is on the phone telling me good luck and Sulien is in front of the house giving me a ride to the test center and then I am in front of the computer and surrounded by cardboard protection and it is only me, as it has been each of the previous four times I have taken this test.

And I breathe and line up the three #2 pencils I have with me and I breathe and I watch the square box on the screen that reads BEGIN and I breathe and I take a small sip of the twelve-ounce cup of water I am allotted and I push the hair out of my eyes and I look up at the clock and over at the woman distributing the test who is popping her gum and reading a magazine as she has each of the previous four times I have taken this test.

And I breathe and the eclipse is happening and my father is humming as I'm in the back of his truck and the triplets are coming out of my body and I am shaking Uri's hand for the first time and I am seeing birds and stars and smelling the glue of my grandfathers' globes on Luce as I hug her and then I press BEGIN.

111

SULIEN: A frog in a well knows nothing of the sea.
URI: But it makes that well its ocean anyway.

110

Last night, after I had faced The Only Person I've Ever Loved for the first time knowing that I loved her, I sat on a rocking chair in the triplets' room and listened to their breathing, looked out the window at the synthetically lighted night, and I let myself imagine. I thought of me and Luce and Sulien and Uri and the triplets and The Only Person I've Ever Loved and everyone at The Demonstration— both the YES side and the NO side—standing in a field at dusk. It was windy but not cold and our hair was blowing everywhere and we were all laughing because there was something unfamiliar coursing through our bodies, which was possibility. And then, it happened: gravity failed and we started rising. It was a slow rise, but we did it, or we let it be done, and there was a recognition that something extraordinary was happening so there was a little fear, but we embraced it. We rose and rose and Sulien pointed down and said, "Look!" And we all did and we saw everything we had known very intimately—the spaces our bodies had occupied and distances we had traversed—we saw everything, but simultaneously. This is what rising gave us, I thought, as I myself looked down. It gave us the gift of seeing everything at once. And then we kept rising farther and we began to see how our town was oriented in the frame of the larger region and we continued rising and we saw just shapes of land and water and we continued rising. We rose very slowly—this was all very slow—and we carefully directed each other around the space material, the fields of rock and burning gas and human-made debris. There were NO people holding the hands of YES people and there were the three tiny humans I grew inside my body and there was the woman who entered existence at the same time as my father and there was the person who taught me friendship and the person who taught me curiosity and we kept rising. And then, released from Earth's crust, on the other side of the sky, we stopped and I told everyone to look. "Look!" I said. "See," I said. I pointed away from Earth. "It is the stars, the naked cosmos," I said. It is a million other universes, pulsing and breathing. It is the wonder of infinite galaxies straight through the retina of the eye.

As I am taking the test, I am thinking of this because last night, in my imagination, that is where I left us. I left us there, on the celestial wavelength of something much greater than anything down here. I left us there, even as we are here on Earth, me in a room with a test, the triplets with Uri at the duplex, Luce in the yard of globes, Sulien with the human-sized nests.

I am taking the test that is the portal to the rest of my life and we are here on Earth but we are also above all of this.

I did not bring us down from there.
We are hovering, still.

109

THE GHOST OF BIRDS: *[Indecipherable.]*

108

I take the test and I go home and I get hugs from everyone and they ask how it went and I do my best to tell them. But I can't really know. I felt like the fourth state of matter—viscous and slippery, not quite solid or liquid or gas—the whole time the test was taking place. I couldn't tell how I was performing and how it was measuring up, this time compared to the last time I took it, the time before that, the second time or the first. I see them look at each other, give each other glances. I see them look at me with eyes that are forlorn. The triplets spend the most time they have ever spent cuddling with me on the couch. I think Uri told them that I needed it, and while I may have confronted him about this in the past, for days I let the triplets' bodies envelop my own, just as my body once enveloped them.

The results I will learn via email, within seven to fourteen days. In the meantime, I can eat again, sleep again, think about the world again without physics. I can think about myself again, inside the world again, not transposed over it. I can feel myself again, walking on the surface of the earth.

The Only Person I've Ever Loved once told me that she did not believe there is life after we die. She thought we were only animals, and that when we ceased to be alive, we would go into the ground and become the earth. She told me this the day after my father died, and I distinctly remember feeling a dual sense of sorrow and relief, this feeling that I was both empty and exhausted, that now perhaps I would not fear waking up. I remember feeling so completely and thoroughly full of a mix of grief and liberation and guilt that she could have said anything and it would have worked to ease that ache. She could have said the same word over and over until it lost meaning and it would have done the work I needed it to do.

She has always known what I've needed, and—for a moment—I wonder if perhaps that is why I loved her. Perhaps, I fear briefly, that is why she remains The Only Person I've Ever Loved.

I am in my bus, and I know my time at the helm will be over soon. Go the opposite direction, she had said. See the same world through a different lens.

The road is wide here, so I don't have to back up the bus—I make a U-turn and I go the way I came. And somehow, like magic, the same course I've been taking for seven years is completely new and strange to me. In a matter of minutes, my town—the town I've never left—is made fully unfamiliar, like walking through a threshold into a mirror world. It reminds me of going into Uri's side of the duplex. I know the blueprint of the place by heart, know every nook and cranny, and yet—at the same time—it feels totally foreign to me.

I drive around like that, over and over the opposite way. The loneliness that lodges in my heart when I'm driving Route 0 seems to lift while I make these strange loops. And I begin thinking. I think of this thing I used to do as a child, when there were still birds and stars. I would stand in the mirror and watch myself, study the mask of my face. I would stand there studying and tell myself, "I am a person. I am a person," over and over again, until something unsettling happened. "I am a person, I am a person," I would say, and I would stare so hard and long that very suddenly, almost instantly, this switch would flip and to my dual satisfaction and horror, I would not recognize myself. I would not understand who it was staring back at me and the fact of me being made of skin and bone and blood on a planet that rotates around a sun and in a world where most things crawl but some swim and billowing vapor lives overhead and there is divorce and soda and we move around in vehicles fueled by liquified dinosaur and there are picnics but there is also murder, and chocolate but also hate. Language, whales, fingers, debt—all of that became surreal, like an unbalanced, off-key fiction someone built. I would be looking at myself in the mirror and in my brain I knew this was me, this thing that is my face the one I've had forever, but in my heart, something felt wrong and ill and off— the fact of me, my face—that I had a face at all—felt otherworldly. Outlandish. Unreal.

I am thinking of this as I drive Route 0 the opposite direction. I am thinking that this experience of not recognizing myself—it is precisely how I have been feeling about The Crisis. In fact, I have been feeling this for a very long time. I see the things around me—the bus, an apple, the triplets—but everything feels irrevocably distorted. Like everything I know has lost some central property that's invisible but also essential.

I think of whether or not this feeling is linked with my father's theory about our imitation world.

I drive, over and over, making rings around my town. There are moments when I start to panic, when my skin grows slick with sweat and my breathing gets uneven. There are moments when I am certain my body is not mine and some ethereal force is pushing the pedal and turning the wheel. And there are moments when I feel in such complete control that I want to abort the next turn and go straight, escape the orbit of this town by leaving everything about it behind me, follow the road directly to whatever comes next.

These are the things I think, the things I feel, and when finally I look at the clock and see my shift is nearly over, I think one last thing. The thing that I think is this: the hummingbird is the only bird that flew backward.

That night, after we eat, I put the triplets in their stroller and I take them to the road that leads nowhere. I let them get out and we walk the road a bit and then we reach the end. But they don't stop when the road stops. They just keep right on going.

I wonder then about all the ways adulthood clips a person's wings. We keep walking and the triplets are in front and I am behind and somehow they walk right to it, like they know. I think of the story of Girl in Glass Vessel, about the fact that adults don't know how to listen to the ghost of birds telling them the tale.

They crouch in front of Saturn and finger the deep cuts in the cement that spell the word, the deep cuts that make the orb's shape. It says Saturn, I tell them. That is Saturn, I tell them and then I tell them that because the cosmos stretch across such great distances, time is measured in light. They look at me then with crinkled brows. They look at me sincerely. Saturn, I tell them, is a bit over one light hour from Earth. That means if we could see Saturn in the sky, what we would see is Saturn an hour ago.

All three of them look up at the sky, and my heart—I can barely stand it. My heart is on the precipice of breaking. For there is nothing up there but the blankness, a flat plane of nothing, like a turned-off screen.

When we get back, the triplets tell Uri I took them to Saturn and he looks at me sideways and I tell him to grab two beers.

107

The night I decided to raise the triplets myself, I weighed my options. My options included trying to give them to someone else here in town, another couple struggling. Or handing them over to Uri, who had never taken care of anyone but himself. Another option was to give them to Luce and cross my fingers. Each possibility ended in the notion of me leaving town for good, leaving them behind to grow up here in my negative space and joining The Only Person I've Ever Loved beyond the limits of this town, wherever it was she had gone. The problem being that I was me.

Because I am me—because that is who I am, a person shaped forever by the hands and minds and hearts of those who have left me—I kept thinking about the past, kept rewinding it, seeing all that had happened to me and reflecting on how it had led here, to this particular now. Then I tried to imagine a future with The Only Person I've Ever Loved, the triplets the trace of a memory, something that happened to me once instead of the center of my life—and that future was laden with guilt and discomfort, sorrow and dismay.

My déjà vu was overwhelming that night, the sense that I had been here before, on the edge of this decision. I willed myself to tell myself what it is I was supposed to decide. I wanted the déjà vu to last that long, to push me into the decision so that when it came, it felt like it had already happened and thus it felt correct.

But déjà vu is all about the future haunting the present, not the other way around. I sat down and thought carefully about the human beings inside of my body then. I tried to feel them kick. I looked out the window and into the sky and then, quite suddenly, on the sill, a cardinal landed. It looked at me through the glass and I looked back at it and it tilted its head and tapped on the glass three times with its beak. And then it did something I will never, ever forget.

The cardinal opened its mouth as far as it could and spread its wings as far as they would stretch and stayed that way, making itself bigger than itself. Trying to expand itself, to stretch and make itself larger than the scaffolding of its body. The feathers were frenzied, split, even the talons of its feet were spread.

Then, just as suddenly, the cardinal collapsed into itself, tapped on the glass three more times, and flew off.

It wasn't the way the cardinal expanded itself, as though to scare off a threat. It was the three taps. Up until then, every time it had come to

me, usually at night when no cardinal would be out, always to a window I happened to be looking out, every time it had come—hundreds
of times since my father died—the beak had only tapped twice.

The cardinal is gone now, as are all the birds, and now when faced
with a difficult decision, I have to make it by myself. I try to listen
to the ghost of birds, like in Girl in Glass Vessel, and though I know
how to listen better than anyone, and though I know that—according to the story—the ghost of birds is curating the tale, my worldly
costume does not permit me to get on that frequency. Though I
know they are speaking it even now, somewhere beyond, I cannot
hear what it is those birds say.

106

I join Uri on a blanket on our tiny front yard, having just checked
my email again. There is no word yet on the results of the test. I think
back on this twilight period I've endured the last four times and remember that there is nothing productive in thinking negatively.

"Good news," Uri says.

"I could use some," I say back, and give him a smile.

"I took your advice." The triplets are playing with Uri's wings
even as he wears them, fingering the bits of paper with notes about
the play and bows of ribbon he's tied on and hunks of bark and chess
pieces and crowns of fresh flowers he's laced through the wire weave.

"When did I give you advice?" I ask.

"I guess you didn't offer it directly. I just sort of borrowed your
mode," he says and when he sees I'm clearly confused, he says: "I
went backward. The way you're always going. I went in reverse. Asked
Luce about the etymology of the word crisis. It comes from Greek
and Late Middle English and means, roughly, the moment of decision, a tipping point, a threshold."

Of course, I already know this, so I nod once, waiting for what comes next.

"Did you know that in the sixteenth century, the dénouement of a play was called The Catastrophe? The Catastrophe—that which follows a crisis, when things lean the wrong way and get worse rather than better."

The skin of my body tightens then, as I think about a variety of things in my life getting worse.

"But this play is about The Crisis," I say.

"Exactly. That's precisely what I realized. We are at the turning point, the moment of going either direction. The play has to stay firmly in The Crisis. It can't get better and it can't reach The Catastrophe," he says.

I nod, take a swig of my beer. "So you're cutting things off in the middle," I tell him. It's a smart decision, I think. Limbo, that place of neither left or right. Limbo, neither YES nor NO. I ask him then what dénouement means, as it's a word I do not know.

"*Dénouement*," he says, adjusting his wings, "means falling action." Uri smiles then and takes a huge slug of his beer, and tells the triplets he has an itch near the tip of his left wing and they giggle as they scratch it and he pretends this gives him great relief.

This is how Uri decides to end the play. He won't let Icarus fall.

105

I had one tape of my grandfathers' voices. It was them narrating—back and forth—a version of Girl in Glass Vessel. Most of the tape had been damaged, so I didn't have them narrating the whole piece—I only had this short part from the very middle of the story. But it is both of their voices: Grandad and PaPa. The tape starts all garbled from the damage to the ribbon—it got wet or melted or maybe someone pulled the ribbon out to sabotage it or maybe it happened by accident—but then their voices fall into the listener's ear and then, after about three minutes, it falls right back into its ruined state.

I remember when I found it, I thought it was a miracle, that their voices were emerging from this record when I believed their voices had been long gone.

On one of his worst days, my father took that tape and what he did with it, I do not know. He died just days after I realized the tape was gone, and then I didn't have time to mourn the tape anymore because I was too busy mourning him.

The section has nothing to do with the Girl in the Glass Vessel—it's all about the planetarium. It's all about the planetarium's loneliness even though it is packed with humans every day, and how it envies the real night sky because it will always be merely and absolutely just a replication.

104

Uri and I are at the field, just a few hundred feet from Saturn. We are checking out the stage. Now that he's written the ending, he is ready for opening night. He and Luce have worked hard at trying to discern the right design. It is minimal, made with recycled material from when The Factory was gutted and repurposed into The Farm. They've decided on a slightly raised platform for Uri to stand on, a large square metal frame, and a set of red curtains that are actually a patchwork quilt Sulien is making from various red materials he's found at the community center's rummage sale.

He never announces it, but somewhere along the way, it is understood that Uri will be playing Icarus.

"Stand back, way back there," Uri says, waving me farther and farther away from him. The stage is imaginary right now, and we're trying to scope out distance and perspective, the actor-audience dynamic, as Uri calls it. "Way back!" Uri is shouting, and I keep backing farther away. Finally, he yells, "Stop!" and I do and he starts in on the beginning of Act 3, which is the quietest part of the play. He finds a way to make it feel like he is whispering while also projecting his voice, and the effect seems impossible. I realize then what Uri means when he says the human body is an instrument. Then he breaks character and yells, "How's it sounding?"

"It's fantastic! But this is about the edge of where the audience can hear," I tell him. "I wouldn't plan on seating folks beyond this point."

"Perfect. Come back," he says, and I walk toward him and see he is writing notes on a bit of paper. Then we do visuals from the left and right—what angle should the curve of the chairs be set at so everyone can see him. He stands on a milk crate for height, since it is about equivalent to the height of the unbuilt stage, and he takes some more notes. Then he shoves the pencil into his left wing and the piece of paper into his right. His wings are full of all kinds of ephemera—buttons and fabric braids, a few photographs.

"Now, for the real work," he says. "Let's go see Saturn."

It's a short walk from his stage to the sixth planet. When we arrive, he walks over, bends down. He runs his hand over the cement block. "Was it this cleaned up when you found it?" he asks and I tell him no, that I did that work. He nods, then walks around it in a circle once, twice, slowly scrutinizing the placement. Then he walks away, into the tall grass beyond where the road ends, pushing the grass aside.

"What are you looking for?" I ask him.

"Nothing," he says. "Anything."

He pulls out his notebook from its typical place, tucked into his left wing near his ear, and pulls a pen from his right. He makes some notes, stops and orbits the cement block again, then jots something else down.

"Okay," he says. And then he looks at me and smiles. "Let me digest this and get back to you with some ideas. How about homemade pizza for dinner?"

103

Sulien is the first to notice when the nests stop going up. We are in the community center and he's moving fluidly between carefully cutting the same-sized squares from red T-shirts and burgundy blankets and maroon towels and pink sweaters and very meticulously hand stitching the various squares together into long bands. For a moment, it reminds me of the strips my grandfathers used to revise their globes.

"Had to know it would stop sometime," he says.

"Don't you want a machine for that?" I ask him. "Seems like it wouldn't take as long."

"Didn't get the feeling from Uri that we were in a hurry."

I nod, since I know that's true.

"Trouble is," Sulien says, "I'm not sure who will take care of them now that it seems the artist has run out of town. I worry," Sulien says, then puts his sewing down and removes his rubber thimble, lifts the scissors to cut up a pair of red denim pants, "that without proper upkeep, they'll go the way of all real bird nests—they'll fall apart."

I hadn't thought about that, and when I do now, I am surprised how sad I am. There was something charged and exciting about the nests, something magnetic. I suddenly cannot imagine our town without them, do not remember our town before they were here.

"Could we do it? Keep them up?" I ask him.

"Very easily," he says, muffled, a needle between his lips as he arranges the squares he's just cut into a long row, begins to pin them together.

"Let's do it, you and me."

He threads his needle. "But your route," he says.

"Won't be long before my route is running without me," I tell him.

He nods and then points to the scissors, and I grab them for him as he ties off a knot on the string.

"Any word about the test?" he asks.

"Not yet," I tell him, and then I let some time pass before I speak again. "Will we ever figure out who put the nests up?"

"I think that depends on how much you want to know," he tells me, and glances at me sideways before returning to his work.

102

THE GHOST OF BIRDS: *[Indecipherable.]*

101

We are in the field and Luce is putting together the theater. She's welded together the square frame that will be the top and sides of the stage back in town, then borrowed a flatbed trailer from The Farm to carry the frame to the field. Now she is building the platform on which the play will unfold.

After she's done, we sit on the platform and look out over the space where the audience will be. The audience will face the field that extends elsewhere, over the horizon. Uri, on stage, will face town. To our left is the road that leads nowhere, and I look over, see the way its end is so abrupt. There is something hidden there that feels like it matters. Then I think of The Only Person I've Ever Loved. I wonder if Luce has ever found someone with whom she could imagine making a life.

Luce lights a cigarette and hands me one, and I use hers to light mine.

"Aunt Luce," I say.

"Yep."

I hesitate for a minute, hovering over my question. I fear that punch of sorrow that comes when a mystery is solved. But I press on: "Have you ever heard a story about the solar system being built over our town?"

"Sure. That one goes way back. They say that buried in the architecture of all this," she gestures around her, "is the whole system that orbits the sun. They say there is nothing but the rest of the universe expanding beyond the town limits. It's just lore, of course, but sometimes when I'm on a particularly long shift at The Farm, I get to thinking that maybe this whole town really is the only system out there, solar or otherwise."

We are quiet for a moment. I can hear the wind through the trees but I cannot hear the birds.

"Aunt Luce," I say.

"Yep."

"There's something I want you to see."

100

The first day the nests appeared and we got in them, after Uri had left to relieve Luce of her shift with the triplets, when it was just me and Sulien, he told me about his partner, how she, too, had died because of complications related to her web of mental illnesses. He left things ambiguous, but he made it clear that no one knew how to help his partner—not the doctors, not the therapists, not himself, and not her. He told me how difficult it was for them to determine what was wrong and give it a name, how impossible it was for them to find a way for her to be treated.

This town, he said, has a gap in the way it deals with mental health.

It was the first time someone had put language to what I'd been feeling all those years with Luce. There was a gap, or maybe it was better to call it an abyss, and my father had fallen in it and Luce and I, we'd fallen in it, too, and maybe, just maybe it wasn't our fault. Maybe falling into that abyss, lingering on the bottom and screaming upward for help—maybe that was a problem on the part of a system, not a failure on the part of a family.

I have never thought about it until now, but sitting in the community center, helping him cut equally sized blocks of red fabric from the clothing and bedsheets and blankets of my fellow townsfolk, spending afternoons this way, not speaking but working together using finger points and nudges and nods toward one thing or another—in this moment, as I hand him a square of scarlet fabric, I realize perhaps it is this shared fact—the fact of losing a family member to mental illness, of feeling the fear of falling into an abyss—maybe that is what makes me care so deeply for Sulien. The human mind is an enigma, and loving someone whose mind is ill is a riddle repeated infinitely, never resolved. Sometimes the only response is what Sulien and I share together, which—for now, for the time being, at least—is ongoing comfortable silence.

99

ICARUS: *[At the window, winged, his father fast asleep.]* No, no. Yes, yes. Yes, no, yes, yes. No, no. Yes. No. No, yes, no.

98

In his performances on the makeshift stage that is the porch of our duplex, Uri doesn't read the stage directions. I didn't even know they existed until I heard Luce read them to the triplets once. They are these incredibly beautiful sections that the audience never gets access to, that are really only for the actors. These parts of the script sort of dissolve in the performance itself, get put into action through the actor, and therefore never get read.

It wasn't until one night when I was listening through the door of their room as Luce read the ever-evolving script to the triplets that I learned just how beautiful they were. I started by putting my ear to the door, but as I listened, I was mesmerized, found myself sliding to the floor. I sat there the whole time she read, listening to the words that would otherwise have gone unheard. The stage directions are supposed to give insight to the actor on what is going on behind the scenes, but since Uri is the only one who has ever performed them, he was the only one who had ever read them until then.

When Luce emerged, I asked her why she'd read them aloud if they were not really part of the play.

"Just because they aren't spoken aloud doesn't mean they aren't part of the play," she told me. "They are still what happens to the actors, what they are supposed to convey—their face and their gait and the language of their bodies. And too, Uri's stage directions—to me, at least—they are a story in themselves."

"But it's just interiority," I told her. "I mean, it's beautiful, but it's just what happens inside the characters' heads. And plays are about the visible, the external. What can be seen."

She shook her head at me then, sighed. She had that look, the look that I should be understanding something about the world that I didn't yet understand. I got the feeling it had to do with something I should be seeing but wasn't, something I wasn't sensing about how I went about being in the world. Like the microwave background in all those years before it was discovered—the key to everything that lingered undetected, just beyond our reach.

97

I watch Uri rehearse and I help Luce build the stage and I help Su-lien sew the curtain and it is all coming together, the play. It is all guise, all fiction—the curtain, the stage, the wings Uri wears on his back. *Costume* and *custom* share an etymology, Luce tells me one day while she's bringing donated clothes for Sulien and me to cut up and sew back together. I think then of old whimsical stories, folktales, how fiction and familiarity are so closely linked. *Cosmetics* and *cosmos* share an etymology, Luce tells me while she's watching Uri apply his makeup. Both have to do with the beauty of order.

I drive my routes around my town and in my downtime, I sit in Luce's yard and watch the worlds spin on their axes.

Limbo is a curious place to be, I think.

YES or NO, I think.

Never, I think, as the worlds move in the wind. Never, I think, or now.

96

The day I get the results it is raining. I open my email, and there lies a message on the top. The subject line makes clear that the digital message will contain my results, but before I press it, I breathe in a few times and push the hair from my eyes and imagine a hug from my father.

I think of my father and I at the lake. He in his bathing suit, his belly fur coiling around his stomach, us splashing each other gently and doing dead-man's float. This was the same lake as the footage I have of Luce and him and their fathers, and because there's more pollution, by the time my father takes me to this lake, there is sea glass to collect. I think of my father's beard, the way he'd grow it out long in the winter months and then let me help him shave it off in the summer, snip the long hair with small scissors until we could see the shape of his chin, then apply the shaving cream so I could run the razor smooth across his cheeks. My father's voice reading to me *Girl in Glass Vessel*. Walking into the house after school and seeing his boots and getting instantly warm all over because he was here, he was home. The way he would cut up my fruit into tiny, perfect squares. The way he would let me paint my own bedroom door with rainbows and flowers and planets. The sound of his laughter when I'd ask him strange, large questions about aspects of the world I did not understand. The smell of his neck as he carried me to bed.

When The Only Person I've Ever Loved would write on my back, as I tried to discern what she was saying, I would think: I wonder if this is what it was like for my father to communicate with his doctors and his therapists and us.

She was writing and with passion, but I could not tell what the writing revealed. I could not tell if she was writing *intention* or *invention*, *future* or *façade*, *destiny* or *design*. I could not tell if she was writing *fate* or *hate*, *father* or *forever*, *birth* or *bird*.

I open the message and there in the center—there are the words and they are bold and clear and written with passion, just like that of The Only Person I've Ever Loved, and I am reading them but I am not comprehending. I am reading the words there but the content of the words seems to escape me. I breathe and I sit on the floor. Then I lie on the floor. Then I roll over and put my face to the floor. I rest my wet cheeks on the cool wood of the lowest place I can possibly go, at least in the physical world.

What is the etymology of *failure*? I think then, but Luce isn't here to tell me.

95

There is a globe in the front yard of the house of my grandfathers that is only ocean. It is just a blue orb with text and lines, a political map designating which sea is which, naming each body of water, delineating where it begins and ends. But nowhere on its surface—nowhere at all—is there a single bit of land. The space where the continents should be is just empty blue, as though the sea rose so high it buried the land underneath it.

Sometimes I think about scratching off the top layer to find whether the continents are there underneath the ocean or if the globe was abandoned mid-construction, the addition of the land forever still to come.

94

THE GHOST OF BIRDS: *[Indecipherable.]*

93

Luce and I are sitting on her front porch, looking over a field of flawed and replicated Earths. I am chain smoking and Luce is lighting each of my new cigarettes as the old one grows low and I crush them into the upside-down northern hemisphere that is our ashtray.

"What happened to working hard and wanting it enough?" I ask her, the tears coming quickly and collecting from both sides of my face at the bottom of my chin.

"Nothing happened. That's what you had to learn yourself. Working hard and wanting it—that was always a fantasy. It was never true. For some people, once, maybe, but not most people now," she says, and she takes out her kerchief with a globe embroidered on it and wipes the tears from my chin.

"I don't believe you," I tell her.

"You don't have to," she says. "I think you are coming to a place where it's got nothing to do with believing me. It's about believing what you yourself know is true."

"How long have you known it wouldn't happen?" I ask her. She gives me a look that says there's no way she's going to answer that.

I shove a spent cigarette into the bottom of the upside-down northern hemisphere and take a new one, already lit, from her hand. "The problem is this, Luce," I say to her, and I shift my body so that I'm looking into her eyes. "I don't know who I am if I am not a radio astronomer. Without that out there on the horizon—without that, I don't know what direction to head."

"But kiddo," she says, and my god, her voice. It sounds just like my father's. "The future's in the same direction. Just keep heading the same way," she says.

I spin the closest globe. "I see your logic, but my whole life I've been either making loops around this town or spinning in place. That's the direction I've been headed. Right back to where I began."

And her face—Luce's face—it looks like her face will break open with sorrow. It looks like her face will collapse with pain. She looks so hurt, so full of some kind of hidden anguish that for a moment I worry more about her future than my own.

"You're going to be okay," she says then, but the way she says it worries me. "You're going to get out of this," she says, and then I am really confused, but when I ask her what she means she is up and gone inside the house.

And then it is just me and the world. Me and the worlds, alone and mourning and smoking. It is me and the worlds—all of us, together— spinning on the axis at the core of each of us, spinning perfectly in place.

92

The evening of Uri's debut, we all gather in the field. Every folding chair is occupied, and some folks bring blankets to sit on the ground. I know so much of the play by heart, I can whisper every word, but by

Act 3, Scene 4, it is all new to me, and despite my ongoing sorrow at my new brush with failure, I am still able to feel the thrill of communal revelation that Uri says only happens when you're watching a play.

The end is what makes the whole thing work. I find it both haunting and full of hope. It's haunting because he ends the story when we all know what is about to unfold. But it's hopeful because by ending it there, the possibility exists that what should unfold will not.

It fills me with a kind of resolve that I can still escape. That I can find a way to get out and beyond all this, like the planetarium that splits itself open to see—for the first and only time—the awe and beauty of the experience it's meant to imperfectly replicate.

Our town loves Uri's play. We insist that it happen once a month, and Uri obliges, has an afternoon run every first Saturday. There is just enough time between the Demonstration in the morning and Uri's matinee that all the people of the town can make both.

Sulien and I spend hours fixing the bird nests as I talk and talk and talk about why I failed, how I failed, what forms my failure took and is taking. He brings me dozens of cinnamon nutmeg chocolate chip cookies, and I cry and eat and smoke and we work on fixing the nests. He is silent and listening. And slowly, over days and then weeks, I begin to find a way not out of my hurt but sort of through it. It's still hugging me, surrounding me, but I can start to—very slowly—I begin to see what's on the other side. Maybe, I realize as we sit in front of the memorial to birds at the community center, as I stand in the field and listen but do not hear birds, maybe there is something on the other side of failure and it isn't necessarily success.

Because our town loves Uri's play, a month after that first performance, we gather to watch Icarus do it all over again: struggle with his father, tell us about the complexities of the labyrinth, fear the height of the tower he's been locked away in, try to anticipate the work of navigating the skies. Once a month we wait for him to take flight and in doing so fall, and each month he stays hovering on the precipice.

The whole town shows up, again and again. I could be wrong, but I feel Uri's performances becoming more intense, more sincere and genuine each time he enters the stage.

After the fourth run of his play, we all walk home together—me and the triplets and Uri. Luce had taken Sulien home in her truck after they very carefully took down Sulien's patchwork curtain. The frame of the stage—the scaffolding—stays up in the field, empty as an abandoned shell.

Each of the triplets wants us to carry them at different points, and so at any given moment, One of them is in my arms, Another is in Uri's, and the Third is between us, holding one of each of our hands. We change out the cycle every three or so blocks.

When we get to the front yard of our duplex, we put them all down and Uri unlatches the fence and we walk through. I tell Uri to let the triplets into my side, and he unlocks the door with his key and grabs the mail, and then I see the lights in my side go on, downstairs and then upstairs and I can hear the triplets squealing as Uri gathers them up in a single scoop and carries them up the stairs. I see the silhouette of them getting into their pajamas through the upstairs window, and I hear Uri telling them to brush their teeth.

Something feels uncomfortable then. On the one hand, I am looking at the building where I live and there in front of me are the people inside it, the people with whom I have made this building a home. But there is also something else I am sensing—that sense of alignment. That things can't stay this way for too long before something will slip, something will change.

Before the curtains opened tonight at Uri's performance, One of the Triplets cupped a small hand and whispered into my ear, "The black hole is coming to get us," but I didn't have time to change the story, couldn't correct this wrong fact. Then the curtains opened and everyone started clapping and we settled into watching Icarus on the edge of the tower, trying to find the right path.

I didn't have time to tell the triplets, no—there is no black hole coming. Because I didn't correct the narrative, now it feels true.

I gather myself. Every step I take toward the duplex—which is full of the sound of the triplets upstairs choosing a book to read, full of the smell of Uri's tea steeping—every step I take toward the place I call home makes me ache.

When I get inside, I see where Uri dropped the mail. There are a few envelopes, including one very thin one, my name written on the front by a human—not typed by a computer—in tiny script with blue ink. I flip it over and fit my thumb under the top and pull it open.

The single sheet says this: my time driving the bus is over.

From here on out, the bus will drive itself.

91

Uri told me once that we make meaning of our lives based on the way we organize our experiences, place events that feel important into a sequence or series that are linked by cause and effect. Uri says "The king died and then the queen died" is just life, but meaning is: "The king died and then the queen died *of grief*."

It's the grief that gives the queen's death meaning. It's that mention of the grief that gives me a small pain in my chest because one event caused another, and that becomes the entrance point to sorrow.

Three clipped knocks come from the other side of my bedroom wall, which is Uri. I knock back three times, which means I'm coming over, and then I go downstairs with the baby monitor and he is already on the porch. He is wearing his wings and they are so full I worry they are doing damage to his back and he shakes his head and says, "The sundial."

And I say, "The sundial?" clearly confused.

He hands me a can of beer and he cracks his open and explains to me that he's done the calculations and if in fact Saturn was found at the edge of the end of the road that leads nowhere, and if you drop the "dial" from the sundial at the center of our town and think of it as The Sun, then the distance between it and the marker called Saturn is precisely 9.58 miles, which wouldn't mean anything except—and he takes a big swig from his beer—9.58 also happens to be the exact distance in Astronomical units between the center of our solar system and the sixth planet, named after the Roman god of agriculture: Saturn.

He smiles an impossibly wide smile and adjusts his wings by wiggling his shoulders and holds out his beer to cheers me. And I nod and look at the ground because everything is aligning, and it is both menacing and magical. I crack open my beer and meet his with mine and then I take long pulls until the can is empty.

90

Precisely one year to the day before the eclipse, the birds were acting strange. I noticed them on the fourth orbit of our town on Route 0. There were great flocks of them above us, but the flocks were composed of a myriad of different kinds of birds—jays and pigeons, robins and chickadees. I stopped the bus at a red light and someone in the back of the bus said, Look! and everyone peered out their windows.

That night as I was dropping off the last of the folks on my route, Sulien moved to the front of the bus. I asked Sulien what it meant, because I knew Sulien knew birds better than any of us.

"Something's coming," he said.

And I said, "Of course—the eclipse." But then I saw Sulien shake his head left to right in the rearview mirror.

"When birds are in danger, they flock together. They'll put aside their differences in size and shape and become a collective. It's a coping mechanism for some forthcoming disaster."

I had looked behind me and let off two people—a NO person

and a YES person—and they scoffed at each other and bickered on their way off the bus. They were the last ones left, except for Sulien, who stayed seated. So I put the bus in park, put on the brake and emergency lights, then turned around to face him.

"I don't see what you are saying."

He scooted a few seats down and leaned as close to me as he could while staying seated. "What I am saying is this: We are in the path of totality, perhaps in more than one way."

89

It is decided—when and by whom, I do not know—that the YES people will pursue the rocky planets and the NO people will pursue the gas. This is, in part, to cut the time to find all the planets in half, but also, in part, to make sure they don't have to run into each other as they do their searching, since the rocky planets are closet to the sun and the gas are further away.

They do their searching on weekends and in between their shifts at work, their family meals, their hobbies and their obligations. They take turns with the shifts, make wide orbits around our town in order to find the planets that linger in the ground.

Now, when I visit Saturn, there are flowers and notes in sealed envelopes and collections of fossils and jars full of sea glass. Saturn was the first to be found, and though I never run into anyone else who visits, every time I swing by Saturn, the offerings are new.

I did this, I think. I am not a radio astronomer, never will be, but I did this small thing. I found Saturn and now, together, our town will find the rest of the planets. I have led my town to find our solar system, the world beyond the world.

Saturn has been here this whole time, my whole life, and it was I who ventured beyond the dead end of the road to find it, compelled by the four times I failed the test. Which led to me failing the fifth.

Cause and effect, I think then. Not cause or effect, but both, linked. Fail and pass, I think. YES and NO.

88

THE GHOST OF BIRDS: *[Indecipherable.]*

87

Mercury is the second to be found. I go to the community center and see a note on the bulletin board. It's a printout of a photograph of another faded blue cement block, this one marked with the word *Mercury* and an orb, tiny but present. Under the photo is a description of where Mercury was found—near the post office. I try to reach back into my brain, and while I can't be sure, I want to say Mercury was the Roman god who transported messages. At the bottom of the bulletin are the names of all the planets. Mercury and Saturn have large Xs running through them.

Then I see the drawing the triplets made and somehow—I don't know how it's happening or why—but it looks to me like the drawing has grown. It looks wider and taller, larger than it once was. It looks to have more birds, or rather more scratchy black Vs, while still maintaining that strange dimension, like a flock where the ones in the center are coming right for me and the ones on the outside are, too, but just further away.

Mercury, I think, and then I remember: on his sandals and on his helmet, for help quickly delivering his messages, the Roman god Mercury had wings.

86

The letter that told me I was done as the driver of Route 0 also informed me of my two weeks of severance pay, a product of the vacation hours I'd let collect over the years. Suddenly, I have gaping chunks of time where I am being paid to do nothing. I should be looking for another job, I know this, but I also know everything that is happening feels like it's happening for a reason, and once all this is done, I'll find more work. *Effect*, I think, comes from the Old French for completion, result. Two weeks, I tell myself. For now, I have two weeks.

I spend much of my time with Sulien at the nests, at the community center reflecting on the Bird Wing, visiting Saturn. And though I knew it would happen eventually, when it does, I am both startled and disturbed.

I am on my way back from the library one afternoon, walking alone, and I see it suddenly coming toward me—the automatic bus. It passes, unaware that I used to be the one running Route 0, that of all the townspeople, I am the one most hurt and confused by this mechanism that is human-less, that is capable of driving itself.

I watch it make a right on Fourth, no one at the wheel.

That, I think, used to be my job. I used to be there, shuttling the people from their homes to the places that housed their needs, to all of their appointments, both casual and formal. I used to lead that route, to manage it, get my fellow persons from one place to the next. I did it safely, and on time, with just the right balance of solemnity and cheer.

When it is past me, I keep watching it, look to see if it slows at the stop sign at the intersection of Elm and High. It does, and then turns right.

There goes Route 0, an empty shell propelling itself forward with no sense of why.

85

"Did you know," Sulien is saying, "that migrating birds used the stars to navigate the night sky?"

"I think I knew that, yes," I tell him.

"Do you know," he says, "how we learned that they did?"

I have to consider this for a minute before I tell him I don't.

"A planetarium. They let some birds go in a planetarium and then they shifted the night sky twenty degrees over and over again, and every time they followed the fake route. Until that point, they'd thought birds only used a leader to discern the right way."

He can read the surprise in my face.

"Those same migrating birds, they could tap into the Earth's magnetic fields," Sulien says. "This fluid in their eyes—it could interact, get entangled with the Earth. Quantum entanglement," Sulien says.

"Would be nice," I say, "to find the right route for yourself by tapping into an invisible force field covering the surface of the planet. Would be nice to take a test and know your future."

Sulien smiles then and we are quiet for a while. I have told Sulien everything about my life, all of the problems and complexities, but I have not told him about my father. I have not shared with him the good and the bad of it, the struggle of it, despite knowing that Sulien might understand. It has been months since Sulien told me about his partner's struggles, sitting in one of the very first nests, but we haven't spoken about it since.

I want to say something about it now, here, to tell him he can tell me what he lost. What he feared. I want to tell him that while our silence is comfortable, it might be discomfort that we need in order for us both to move forward, like the birds and the invisible force field around the earth.

"Your partner," I say. I say it very gently, very quietly.

Sulien shakes his head at the ground. "Grief," he says, then looks at me. "Is strange. I can't—" He sighs and looks up at the giant nest before us. "Not yet. I can't. Talk about her," he says, "yet."

I nod my understanding.

When I was young, The Only Person I've Ever Loved and I would sit in the bed of my father's truck with our backs to the cab and watch the world that was, the passing, past-tense world, slim down from everything around us to an ever-disappearing point. We would lean against the glass of the truck's cab, and I could hear my father laughing slightly or humming to the radio and sometimes I would turn around and sneak a peek into the cab and I would see him looking out over the terrain of our town, and then I would look back at where we'd just been, and it was moving ever further away from where we were.

The Only Person I've Ever Loved and I would sit side by side, and while we never spoke about it, it was these moments—watching things smear and stretch and move and grow tiny and far away while it seemed she and I sat perfectly still together, the world morphing around us—that convinced me I could not wake or sleep or eat or walk or be or live without her. We were, the two of us, the axis around which the whole world twirled.

Maybe that is an inkling of a fraction of a bit of what Sulien and his partner had together. She was also from the town in which he was born, the one his family was forced to leave. That kind of devastation—finding the town in which you live is no longer a place, only a memory—it must cleave people together in ways I'll never know.

"Were the birds here different than the birds in the town in which you were born?" I ask Sulien.

He stops what he is doing and looks at me with a face that is full of resignation and sorrow. He brings his hands to his chest and breathes deep. He turns his face up, shakes his head. Then he looks at me and smiles.

For the rest of the afternoon he tells me stories. About the trees and the sounds and the grass and the smells and the roads and the food and the fear and the joy and the birds—all the birds, none of which I have seen—all the birds that left him a little sooner than they left the rest of us.

84

[Indecipherable.]

HER GRANDAD: […] is always within the structures of its very being—its curving top and seats that recline, its inherent commitment to dark—the longing to be real, to be the night sky naked, stars not curated lights but the centers of celestial systems beyond any yet-invented measurement. The longing to be real, not an artificial construction wedded to a kind of vertical theater. The planetarium tells its story down, trying to install in all those tiny visages looking up that they are infinitesimal, barely registered in the grand scheme of the sky.

HER PAPA: The planetarium dreams that it splits its top in half, peels itself open and flat against the earth. The cement would have to go soft, the rock skeleton lax, such that it could bend its interior out, turn its captive lamps up, like an open book. The planetarium imagines each point of light on its flat plane matching those suspended in the night. Though perhaps, the planetarium thinks, this would only mimic in a new way, make the planetarium less a sky and more an ocean, the symmetry between real and artificial collapsing one into another until the horizon is lost. At least this act would allow the planetarium to reach the state it most desires: to be outside itself.

HER GRANDAD: The planetarium dreams, but still the people pack into its gut and look up. The human voice hovers, conveying the laws of the primeval world, and it strikes the planetarium as anachronistic or mistaken. A human voice tells about a time without humans, before humans, though, the planetarium thinks, time is human, too. The planetarium's star theater brightens the faces of the people below, and it is at these moments when it reflects on what it knows: that it is just a cage for content, not a portal to beyond.

HER PAPA: A disembodied voice gives names to vapor shapes, but the planetarium knows: when it comes to that which the planetarium only imperfectly reflects, the human mouth and mind fail absolutely.

HER GRANDAD: It is at night when the planetarium—silent and dark and off—feels most at liberty to ache. The pain is grueling, and this is how the planetarium knows that every simulation is anchored to that which it imitates. It is at night when the planetarium wonders if that spectral tether to Before, umbilical-like, is the planetarium's hurt to bear alone, or if this is the source of all the universe's sorrow [...]

[Indecipherable.]

83

THE GHOST OF BIRDS: *[Indecipherable.]*

82

I had a father and I have him still.

My father is a father who saved up enough money to buy me a real—if secondhand—pair of binoculars to study the stars. A father who showed me so very many versions of Girl in Glass Vessel that I came to be amazed the story was so elastic, could be stretched in so many ways. A father who loved Luce, who shared a private twinhood with her after I was in bed, when I could hear the two of them laughing and cracking open beers on the other side of my bedroom door, in the space that served as both living room and kitchen in our apartment.

At night, I look up from bed to see my star charts on the ceiling and, in my father's handwriting, the date of the eclipse.

Castles in the air, he used to tell me, aren't safe. Beware of fantasy. But these days I wonder where on that spectrum of the real and the imagined lies that tricky thing called hope.

81

The NO folks find Uranus just before the sixth iteration of Uri's play. They find it by the waste management building. I see the announcement on the bulletin board of the community center when I swing by one Saturday morning after The Demonstration. There it is, on the board: a huge map of our town, the sundial in the middle, and the waste management building right along the orbit of the seventh planet. Someone has used a red crayon connected to a compass to draw rings that represent eight orbits, which are all to scale with the actual solar system. It strikes me then, looking at that map, how extraordinarily orb-like our town is, as though the municipal plans were crafted based on these concentric round paths.

There is another board right below it with a ribbon down the center, splitting it in half. One side is dedicated to reports from the NO folks and one side to reports from the YES.

It is a Saturday so I am alone at the community center and I sit on one of the folding chairs and look at the Bird Wing. The community-curated display has expanded, and I feel a wave of sorrow as I come to understand that all our bird narratives live here now. They live here and some of them live in the nests and in our minds and hearts, and that is it. Nowhere else does the memory of birds persist.

I let myself take it all in—the colored pencil chart of different beaks and the printout of flight patterns of migrating birds and a real nest in a shadow box. There are bits of paper with sketches, photographs, a posterboard full of a variety of different single feathers, some glued, others taped.

Then, in the middle of the display, I see the triplets' portrait. Somehow it gets more disturbing with time, and somehow—I must be seeing things wrong, seeing things that are smaller somehow expanding in my brain—somehow the portrait seems to be growing. I know the paper was smaller, I know there were fewer of the scratchy black Vs that constituted birds. It feels impossible, and yet, the frame of the image seems to be swelling, so that the portrait is taking up more of the wall.

Uranus, I remember, also has rings, like Saturn, though more faint. And, I remember then, keeping a close eye on the portrait the triplets made, Uranus is the only planet that spins on its side, its rings running up and down.

80

The yard of my grandfathers—now the yard of Luce—is a three-mile walk from the duplex, but I walk fast and can make it in under an hour. I sit on her porch waiting for her to return from work and listening to the breeze move through the trees.

I think about all that has unfolded on this porch. I think of time—the order of events, the duration of a single memory, the frequency of an event happening over and over again, so that it is both singular, like The Demonstration, and also a kaleidoscope of different days.

Twenty years ago for thirty minutes, my father and I played cat's cradle where I sit now. Thirteen years ago for a whole afternoon, The Only Person I've Ever Loved and I smoked candy cigarettes here, talk-

ed about my dream of radio astronomy and hers of being an architect. Six years ago for an hour, Luce and I sat here and discussed my
father's illness. Two days ago for fifteen minutes, Sulien and I sat here
perfectly silent, waiting for Luce to come out of her house and for
the three of us to walk to the stage in the field to set up for Uri's play.

I can feel the dread in my veins. It is all time, ticking down,
adding up. I start thinking of The Crisis and who built the nests and
the strangeness of the triplets and the ghost of birds and Saturn and
Earth. I start thinking of all the sound, all that sonic information
that is weaving its way through the atmosphere, the sonic information that could be informing us of all the celestial threats, or all the
celestial gifts, and how I am not now nor ever going to gather and
track it, discern an asteroid en route from a new and hungry black
hole, discern the technosignature of an ancient and long-gone society
giving us the answer to The Crisis.

The globes in the yard of my grandfathers are many, and I am
comforted by the knowledge that time might be smaller on those
worlds, too. I will myself to believe that on every one of those globes,
Now has not yet arrived, and if you look closely—if you squint—you
can see great flocks of birds orbiting those worlds. The birds are singing on those worlds and love is being offered and received and people
are holding hands and sharing and failing and learning and breaking
and helping each other put themselves back together.

I stand and look up and there is the sun, which is a star. Then I
pull out the two-way radio from the front pocket of my overalls and
turn the volume up.

79

Venus and Mars are found by the YES folks one day after the other.
They'd been keeping a close watch, and because the rocky planets

have smaller orbits, they were able to do a good deal more laps.

Sulien and I are standing in front of the American robin nest, working on mending the base where things have gotten a bit worn down. He is telling me that the YES folks are now solely focused on Earth.

"What's odd," he says as he reaches his hand out for more of the heavy hay we're using to re-enforce the base, "is that they've been working the Earth orbit hardest since the beginning. They've put twice the number of YES folks on its route. It's strange to know now that it will be the last one they find."

I nod my agreement.

"Unless they don't find it," Sulien says, and we are quiet for a while.

The base of the American robin nest is almost finished, our work nearly done, when he turns to me suddenly and asks: "How long has it been since we've seen stars in this town?"

I weave some more hay through a side of the nest. "A decade. Maybe more."

"I've been thinking about these nests," he says, looking up. "Been thinking, too, about the triplets. Would be nice to show them the night sky."

"How would you do that?" I ask him. "How could that happen, here?"

"If we go the Uri route," Sulien says, and he hands me some more hay and pats the nest twice as if the decision's been made.

78

There are many versions of Girl in Glass Vessel.

As with most stories that have lasted ages, carried by the mouths and voices of those now long gone, there are many different iterations that mutated over the centuries, those mutations happening because of value systems and culture, geographic region and in which era it was told. Because of this, there isn't a definitive, singular text.

Sometimes the Girl is caught not in a clear vessel but in a disguised shell.

Sometimes the planetarium is actually a large cage, on top of which are painted faux stars.

Sometimes the ghost of dead birds curating the story is the voice of a flock of starlings or crows or sometimes a single bird—a hummingbird, sometimes a crane or stork, other times a lark or a jay—who has been killed by the glass vessel in which the girl is caught.

Sometimes the glass vessel isn't glass at all, but transparent, like the invisible shield of Earth's atmosphere.

What there always is—what persists in each telling—is this: a woman constrained by a contraption that's trying to protect her, fake stars, dead birds, and the looping nature of the tale, the story that tells itself, the answer to the question a question itself, like that old riddle about which came first, the chicken or the egg.

77

The problem, Uri is telling me, is that every time he performs it, he is a little bit older, a little bit different, and so it's never quite the perfect show. It's the human element, he says, that is introducing the error. "It's almost like what I need," Uri says, lifting each of the triplets out of the yellow warbler nest and onto the ground, "is to create a play without actors."

76

The problem, Sulien is telling me, is that a whole generation might never see the stars. All this playacting of Uri's has got him thinking.

"If someone can build these nests from essentially nothing, then I can build the night sky," he says.

75

The problem, Luce is telling me, is that she's hearing strange things from those in upper management. She thinks they're suggesting big changes at The Farm, radical, tectonic-level shifts. "I'm worried we're headed down the wrong path," she says.

"The path of totality," I say, and she frowns at me while she runs her hand over her shaved head.

74

THE BUS THAT DRIVES ITSELF: *[A low, persistent hum. Shifting gears. The soft grind of the brakes.]*

73

The day the NO folks find Jupiter it is raining. Sulien and I spend that afternoon in the community center trying to make a schedule for caring for the nests.

"Jupiter, god of thunder," Sulien says. "Strange they found it on a day when it was storming." He looks at me with a sideways look, like I should be thinking harder about this than I am. I feel him wanting me to understand something but I don't.

Sulien is mending a tear in the curtain that splits reality from fiction on Uri's stage. The way he mends the tear makes it look like a huge swath of the curtain has a large scar. He puts the needle through the fabric and pulls it through with his other hand, then does the opposite, back and forth. It reminds me of the common tailorbird nest, the extraordinary work the bird must have done to complete that kind of home. The work that is uncannily like human work. Sulien looks up at me watching him, pauses.

"Guess that just leaves Neptune for the NO folks," I say.

"And for the YES," Sulien says, "Earth."

72

Sometimes, when I am at the end of a bad session of déjà vu, right when I know it's going to stop, when I start to feel that I'm not sure what is about to happen, and therefore that I have returned to regular living when everything to come is firmly unknown, I wonder if my father should have been born a bird from the beginning, never taken human form. Perhaps then he would not have been burdened with all the stupid, beautiful, ugly, stunning, horrifying, gruesome responsibility that comes with being self-conscious.

But yesterday Sulien told me that corvids could recognize themselves in a mirror, and I thought: every living thing crafts its own trap.

71

I hear the talk at The Demonstration.

When I'm on the NO side—surrounded by their pessimism and gloom—they tell me how hard they've been trying: tripling up the eyes on each route, running them twice as often, but surely it's a lost cause.

On days I demonstrate for the YES, they tell me—with a confidence and brightness that borders on naïve—that they've been struggling with finding Earth but find it they certainly will.

On neither side do they talk about destruction, that perhaps these planets have been accidently dug up or pulverized in the time between their being planted in the ground and now.

The bulletin board at the community center got too small to catalog all the intel that was being collected and shared, so the YES folks bought two boards and lined them one on top of the other on the left and the NO folks bought two boards to put up on the right. Within days the boards were full of reports and bits of new information—who had checked where and who had double-checked, what land had been covered and what still needed a fourth look, a sixth.

There was no talk at all that the planets might be present, but could have been on a different lap, whoever planted them there using the wrong measurements.

There was no talk at all that perhaps these planets simply hadn't been planted.

On Saturdays, after The Demonstration, as I am walking home, I think about whether or not I should help.

But the problem of what kind of person I am—if I am a YES or NO person—becomes amplified when I consider the concentric circles both sides are making around our town. So I decide to ask Sulien.

Leave the ground to the young townsfolk, he tells me, and help him with the sky.

Somehow he has a way of telling me just what I need to hear.

70

There is a flawed globe in the yard of my grandfathers that spins the wrong way. The two holes that designate the axis are directly on the equator, so that the north and south poles live to the east and west. When you spin it, what you see are the poles moving from left to right and back again, blurring into each other, no longer poles at all. It is as if someone pulled the invisible rod from the center of the earth and pierced it through the equator.

When I see this globe in particular, I am reminded of the revision happening not only on the globes in the yard of my grandfathers, but on the globe right under my feet.

Revision, Luce tells me, comes from the Latin for *revisere,* "to see again." But I didn't need her to tell me that. The meaning is right there in the word.

One should recognize when the obvious solution is staring one in the face.

69

THE GHOST OF BIRDS: *[Indecipherable.]*

68

Sulien sets up the star house in the middle of the field, next to Saturn.

He is drilling holes in the board that will be both the ceiling of the star house and also, or rather, instead—with a bit of imagination—the night sky.

Sulien is telling me about the planets that are left and where they might be found while he is mapping out—to scale—the distance between the stars in the sky so that the full range of constellations will be visible from the ceiling of the star house.

Early on, Sulien tells me, before there were planetariums because this was before humans knew there were planets, star houses were the low-fi model for learning about what lies above. The house is essentially a large black box, about the size of a one-car garage or the entirety of the duplex's living area and kitchen—with every possible crevasse for light to peek through eliminated. Then, in the top, Sulien will drill holes at different widths that correspond to the night sky. It's the sun that will do the work of illuminating the stars, just like in a real evening. Except in the star house, you can only enter during high noon, when the sun is at its brightest, and then you'll look up and see night.

Most of the younger generation of our town—including the triplets—have never experienced stars. They've seen photographs, of course, but a photograph is nothing compared to the experience of looking at the dome of the rest of the universe above you so that you are reminded that the earth beneath your feet is curved. There is simply nothing like looking up and knowing that there is so very much above you, so very much beyond you, and in knowing that, realizing how infinitesimally small you are in the story of the world. There is something important in that act—in knowing you are trivial, in knowing that the solar system doesn't revolve around the Earth but the Sun, that even our solar system isn't the center of the galaxy but in one of the four arms of the spiraling Milky Way.

Because, of course, at the center of our galaxy is Sagittarius A, a supermassive black hole.

Sulien is drilling into what will become the sky of the star house. I watch him work and think of his life and all he has seen and known and loved and lost. I think of what the stars would have looked like from the town in which he was born.

I think of sitting in this field with The Only Person I've Ever Loved, passing my binoculars back and forth between us during a meteor shower.

That night I swing by Saturn and it is amazing—people have put flowers and hand-stitched blankets and someone, to my astonishment, has left a small globe. The globe is clearly the work of my grandfathers. It has their signature look.

Weeks have gone by, and while there is much new data posted on the bulletin boards in the community center, there's no sign of Neptune or Earth. When I bring this up with Luce, she ignores me, lost in her own thoughts about, I assume, The Farm and whatever is unfolding there, the changes she clearly doesn't like.

"Luce," I ask her, "do you hear me?" But she is lost, elsewhere. So I ask her again: "What is the etymology of *etymology*?"

She looks at me with confusion, then anxiety, then resolve. "I don't know," she says. "I don't know." She runs her hand over her shaved head and then she whispers it over and over as we watch the worlds in her front yard spin.

67

The morning after I help Sulien begin the star house, when I walk into the community center, I notice something strange on the bulletin board.

The four boards that had been recording the progress have all been mashed together to create a single display. While the YES side still has reports of the rocky planets and the NO side reports of the gaseous, toward the center, in the middle, when I try to read the separate updates about Neptune and Earth, to my confusion and astonishment, they seem to overlap and integrate.

I run my finger along the center, starting from the top, but as I move down, I can't discern which side is which.

The triplets' picture is growing, expanding, stretching. I think then of the etymology of *intent*, intention. What we intend.

I wonder about the Girl in Glass Vessel. I wonder about the last moment of her life.

I wonder if she was in awe or if she was scared beyond reason when she faced the world, for one fleeting moment, with no protection at all.

66

Luce and I are sitting on my porch, the triplets down for a nap. We are listening to the sound of space from the baby monitor and we are listening to the sound of the wind through the trees. Together, we are listening.

Luce starts talking, and I have an extraordinary sense of déjà vu, the kind that has been visiting me often lately—the kind that feels like it will knock me out. It starts like this: The way my ankle is draped across my thigh, the angle of the handheld two-way radio in the front pocket of my overalls, the exact color of the sky, the smell of the leftovers from the dinner Uri made sitting unlidded in the Tupperware on the counter, cooling off. The way Luce fingers the notch at the top of her ear. The shape of Luce's face as she grimaces. The sound of Luce's voice drifting across the porch, and also what she says: The Farm is being sold to A Conglomerate.

All of this is happening and then all the movement around me grows very slow while Luce's voice grows very fast. It is as though the sound is not synced with the visual realm or like two parts of my brain are operating independently. The trees slow their pull by the wind so that they look lethargic, a car driving by is crawling and the wave from the hand of the person in the passenger's seat moves like the air is molasses. A smile slowly forms on the face of that person and then, just as slowly, surely as a result of the face I'm displaying back, the smile turns into a frown.

Meanwhile, sped up and orbiting around me is Luce's voice: she has been telling me that now, under this new direction of The Conglomerate, no one will know the nature of what the servers are for. She will not be able to know what, nor who, she is serving. She is unsettled by this secrecy. She is doing this work that she does not understand, she is telling me, this work that she is not privy to, and she feels less like a person and more like a utensil, an appliance or tool. She doesn't know what the hell she is doing. Her voice is growing in volume and moving into higher registers. What is she doing? She is asking me. What the hell is she doing? And am I listening? Am I listening to her? Have I heard anything she's said?

I break from my trance, and though the déjà vu continues, I hold the knowledge of the new-known in the back of my head so that I can tend to Luce with the front.

"Of course I'm listening. Calm down," I tell her. She lights another cigarette, picks the fraying hem of her pants. She runs her hand over her shaved head.

"Calm down," I say, and she puts up her hands in defense, sucks the cigarette hard. And then I ask her what she wants to do.

My déjà vu—it is so overwhelming that I have to close my eyes. I know what she will say not before she says it but at the same time as it comes out of her mouth.

"I want to quit," she says, and when she says it, the look on her face suggests she is surprised. "I want to quit," she says again, as though to herself, as though she is alone.

One should always be honest with oneself, I think then, and the static from the handheld two-way radio in my pocket amplifies in volume just a bit.

As I say what I say, the déjà vu, it haunts me. I know I was meant to say this.

"Make globes," I say, just like that. "Make worlds," I say, and my blood aches with the knowledge that everything is aligning just the way whoever is in charge—which is not me, not me by a long shot—everything's aligning as whoever is in charge thinks it should.

65

ICARUS: *[His father having already taken flight.]* Yes, no. No, yes. No, yes, yes, no. Yes, yes, no, no. Yes, yes, no.

64

After Luce leaves, I give the monitor to Uri and take a long walk to clear my head. But as I'm approaching the sundial, I squint my eyes because I cannot be seeing what it is I am seeing.

There are two people before me. One of them is a NO person, and the other is a YES.

I approach very cautiously because they are next to each other, they are adjusting each other's hats and sharing—can it be?—they are sharing a bottle of water. They are chatting casually, and I think I see one laugh.

"Hi, there," I say as I approach. They do not look to be in peril, which was my first thought. Seeing them here together in this warm way makes me think reality has gone soft. NO and YES people do not spend time together as a rule, other than at The Demonstration when they are disagreeing.

"Well, hello!" they say.

I need to venture lightly. "Everything okay here?"

"Of course! We're gearing up to look for the last two planets," they say to me. "Want to join us?"

The surprise in my mind must take shape on my face because they can read it. One looks at the ground and one looks at the sky and then at the same time they look at each other and nod.

"There are some things," one of them says, "that are not about NO or YES."

"There are some things," the other one says, "that are about the space in between."

I squint at them, shake my head in confusion, and they turn around to reveal one word in very bold font on the back of both of their shirts.

The word is MAYBE.

63

"What is strange to me," The Only Person I've Ever Loved once said, "is that one rotation of the Earth gets us right back to where we started."

We were at Luce's, surrounded by her yard of flawed globes. "The only difference," she said, helping herself to another candy cigarette, "is time."

62

"From the beginning," Uri says. He is rehearsing, and I watch him stop mid-play and move backward in time, instantly erasing all of his mistakes.

"From the beginning," Uri says, and we start all over again.

61

Sulien and I are walking to the field where Uri's theater and Saturn lie, balancing in our arms the charts from my youth to help us with the star house ceilings. As we make our way to the field, we notice long lines of people out in the distance, looking to the ground.

"It's along that course where Neptune should be. They are going to find it," he tells me with a look that doesn't seem so sure. He
explains that they've quadruple-checked the calculations for the exact
distance from the sundial to Neptune—on the adjusted scale—and
used up all the year's allotment of the community center's chalk, usually reserved for making baseball diamonds over at the field, to sketch
in Neptune's orbit.

"If the scale is right," Sulien is telling me, "and if whoever placed
the planets there did it correctly, and if the planets haven't been removed or damaged, then somewhere along that chalk line should be
Neptune."

"Sulien," I say then, "have you noticed that they're—" I stop
myself because I don't quite know how to say it. I'm not sure how to
put what has happened into words. "Have you noticed that they've…
united?"

We've arrived at the star house, halfway erected in the field. Sulien
uses a flathead screwdriver to pry open the lid of a gallon of black paint.
Today, we're starting in on the ceiling that will be the sky in autumn.

"The formerly YES and NO people," I say. "Did you see that
many are now MAYBE people?" He gestures with his head toward
the other paint brush and I pick it up, put it into the can, smear some
of the excess paint off and start in on the board. "It's strange. Or
rather, it's not strange—it's just unusual for this town. In some ways
it's actually normal." I am pulling the brush along the sky, making
it night. "They have this new demeanor. They don't seem quite fully
YES, seeing the glass always, unendingly half-full, but they also—all
of them, or rather none of them—they also don't seem quite NO,
finding and focusing exclusively on the negative, seeing the glass half
empty. Something has changed. Is changing," I tell him, dipping my
brush into the paint again.

I close my eyes for a moment, and before me is the empty bus
driven by no one. Then, for a fraction of a second, I wonder why I
can't hear any birds.

I look off to the distance, and I see the long line of people that is my town. They are hard to see, very small, but I stand to get a better look. They are the size of ants, but there is no denying it—they are walking, mostly single-file though sometimes in twos in a line that stretches from as far as I can see on the left to as far as I can see on the right.

And even from here, this distance, I can read it in their gait, in the way they hold their bodies—the only people in that line are people who are neither YES nor NO. Walking in that line, I can see it—there are only MAYBE people.

I laugh then, and Sulien asks what I find funny.

"It's just that the MAYBE people, they're going the wrong direction. The planets don't rotate that way."

"What way's that?" Sulien asks.

"They're going clockwise. But the planets rotate around the sun *counter*clockwise," I tell him, "and all of them, mysteriously, on the exact same plane."

60

Luce and I haven't spoken about her work since that day I had a bad bout of déjà vu. Luce is not a talker, but she is a thinker, and I resolve that her silence about The Farm has to do with thinking through her next steps.

She is pulling up now. I can hear Uri running the lines of the play from his side of the duplex while the triplets and I are on the porch, tracing shapes into the dust that settles there. The triplets make a series of circles and call them black holes. I am drawing trees, and we can hear Uri and then, I see One of the Triplets mouth the words Uri says aloud. Then, with the next line, I see Another of the Triplets mouth it, too, and finally The Third of the Triplets mouths along as well. They are silently speaking the words, and in this way, they each become Icarus.

I remember then why Uri decided on the Icarus play to begin with. He said it was about being careful with your ambition. The story of Icarus is about finding the middle path, the path of moderation. It's about sustainability, he said, and when I consider the play he's made from it, the play we watch the first Saturday of every month, I realize how far away from that story the version he presents has gone.

Luce gets out of the truck and picks up all three triplets and spins them around in circles, over and over, until their squealing can't be ignored. She puts them down and wobbles a bit getting her balance back. When she's got it, she returns to her truck as she says, "Tried making a globe."

I am surprised, but also not.

"You did? That's fantastic. How'd it go?" I ask.

"Looks like I made a flawed one," and she pulls from the cab of her truck a globe.

It's more than flawed, I realize as she approaches—it seems to be missing whole continents. She hands it to me and I spin it and that is when I realize what she's done.

It's a political globe, but the continents are smashed into each other, all combined into one huge block of land.

"Luce," I say, trying to hide my astonishment.

"Didn't know I could make something round," she says.

I spin the globe. It's Pangea, the first great landmass, but formed of the continents now—their shapes stretched and reframed so that they all fit together. I can't tell if it is beautiful or if it is horrifying, but I let it live in the space between. Earth is here, this, and also completely not. Earth is one huge block of land surrounded by water.

"Tried to capture both the past and the present at once," she says.

"You have, Luce. You really have."

Then Aunt Luce—the person with whom my dead father shared a womb, Aunt Luce, my father's twin—she grabs the triplets and starts gently wrestling them to the ground. They go wild giggling and laughing and snorting and squealing with her.

Girl, bad, curse, bird, I think, and turn up the volume on my two-way radio.

59

[The sound of skylarks have been heard for forty minutes. Throughout what follows, they persist in their calls and singing in the background.]

HER FATHER: Hey there kiddo. It's dawn and the sun is just peeking over the horizon, but the stars are still in the sky. You're sleeping but when you wake up you'll be ten, a decade old. We'll spend the morning at the park, and Sulien made cookies which we'll eat this afternoon at Luce's to celebrate your ten years.

I want to say—I'm making this tape, see, or rather, I guess, hear—I'm making this to say a thing that is somewhere between an apology and a warning. Lately, I just don't feel right. Haven't for a while. Derealization, they say, or depersonalization, I guess. Don't know if it's me or the world. Figure it's both. But I'm not one for labels. Learned that from your grandfathers and Luce. Never felt right being forced to choose YES or NO.

I want to explain it the best I can so you know. In case. In case—in case you need to know.

Everything is off and the only way I can figure why—the only thing that gives me comfort—is knowing that something larger, this thing bigger than you and me, it's mediating our world. I wouldn't call it anything at all except maybe a coating or layer or trace, maybe a veil, a kind of dull knowledge in the back of my skull that means the lens through which I see things is different than it used to be. What I know, though, is that the larger thing will not interfere. It will just hover on another plane above us, before us, watching what it is we choose to do. Like the dead birds in that old folktale about the girl trapped in the invisible eggshell that both protects and constrains her. The dead birds are just curating the story. They would never intrude on what gets said.

Tape's running out, I see the ribbon's just about gone, but I want to say more. I think about the eclipse a lot these days. Today you'll be ten but when the eclipse comes you'll be in your twenties and I will have to find a way to be more proud of you than I am now. I don't want to alarm you, but I also want to give you some advice, the kind I can't tell you directly because—because I'm me.

The advice is not to get trapped. Find a way to break out. If you know what I mean, then do it and do it now, do it quickly. If you don't, then you've never been or you've already escaped.

Tape's running out and I hear you upstairs—you're awake. You have woken up every morning for a decade. The cookies Sulien made are cinnamon nutmeg chocolate chip. Can you hear the skylarks? *[A silence as he lets the birds be heard.]* They are so vibrant today. Can't imagine a world without them. My god, what a wrong world that would—

[Tape ends abruptly.]

58

On my way to help Sulien fix the nests, I run by Saturn. Saturn was found on the edge of a prairie that used to be an old farm. Saturn, god of sowing and seed.

"Do you think," I ask Sulien as we are tending the weaverbird nest, "that there could be a pattern? Saturn, god of seed, was found at the edge of the old farm. Mercury, god of communication, was found near the post office. Uranus, god of rain, found near the water tower. Could there be some connection?"

Sulien's eyebrows rise and I see his cheeks flush. Something strikes him—I can see it in the way his hands hover, hesitating. "What is it?" I ask him. "What did you realize just now?"

He sits for a minute, holds one hand with the other. The look on his face says it isn't something he's realized but something that I have. "Well—it's just that each planet is precisely to scale in its distance from the sundial. But each planet is also wedged into a part of our town that corresponds with the meaning of the god after whom the planet was named."

I stare at him, not comprehending.

"Their location. It aligns with the meaning of each god. But they are also to mathematical scale. It's almost—well." I put my hand over his hands which are gripping each other now. I feel him want me to understand something, understand it on my own. But I cannot. I need his help. He waits a beat and then sighs. "It's almost as if the town was built over the system instead of the other way around."

I walk home the long way and see some MAYBE people doing their orbits, chatting casually and smiling as they scan the ground. They are the MAYBE people, I think. And this town was in the path of totality. And we are in the middle of The Crisis, trying to avoid The Catastrophe.

They are the MAYBE people, I think, and then I think—it's less a question, and more a statement—what kind of person am I.

57

HER TWO-WAY RADIO: *[Static.]*

56

When we were thirteen, The Only Person I've Ever Loved and I were waiting for the bus near Luce's house when she asked me to promise her we would one day leave this town.

"This town," she said. "Promise me we'll leave it."

"We'll leave! We really will," I told her and offered her my pack of candy cigarettes. "I don't want to have to choose between YES and NO."

"It's not that," she said, and she put a candy cigarette in her mouth. "It's harder for women. To leave, I mean," and she looked me right in the eye. "I don't want to be a story. I don't want to become part of this town's story," she said then, and her face got swollen and red and her eyes teared up.

"You won't," I told her, and handed her my handkerchief. She fingered the tiny embroidered globe in the corner, wiped her eyes. Then she sighed really loudly and asked me how much of our lives I thought we'd already wasted waiting for the bus to arrive.

55

"Where's Neptune?" the signs say—the ones covering the sundial, all over the doors of the businesses in town. Yesterday, I saw signs posted in each window of the bus that drives itself, not a soul on board.

"Find Earth," the signs say at the community center, and the triplets' picture grows.

54

Uri's play has been received with great enthusiasm for the duration of its many-month run, but for some reason, he is growing increasingly unsatisfied with his performances.

"Seems to me," I tell him, "you are a marvel. Sometimes I can't tell where you begin and Icarus ends."

Uri says thanks, but he's not looking for compliments. It's about more than that. It's about what the play is saying about The Crisis. The problem, Uri keeps telling me, has been telling me for three weeks now, is that because Uri is changing, then Icarus is also changing, and those changes mean the performance is always an imperfect replication of some perfect performance that can never really be attained.

"What does that have to do with The Crisis?" I ask him.

"What do you mean?" He looks a bit unkempt. "What I'm describing is the very core, the nucleus of The Crisis," he says, his voice straining. His wings are so full of ephemera barely any light can come through.

For a moment—for just one moment—I get a wave of nausea because something strikes me, something I've never thought before.

What if The Crisis Uri and I are talking about is not the same crisis? What if The Crisis when funneled through my mind means something different than The Crisis when channeled through his?

What if The Crisis—my god, my head is swimming, the beating of my heart won't slow—what if The Crisis is not a single crisis, but a series of crises, a web of crises different for every single person on this Earth? Nearly nine billion different crises—one for each human— that are networked and interlocking? And what if thinking of these disparate crises as The Crisis is the first time we've found a way to come together to collaborate as a planetary team about how to begin to solve the nine billion crises within the souls of every person that walks this orb? The nine billion crises that have—in this historical moment of Earth teetering on a tipping point because of greed and cruelty and not thinking about the future but only the present and calling it destiny instead of calling it doom—coalesced. Coalesced, I think, sweating, into a single, Global Crisis.

I sit down then, because I feel my blood ache, my body weaken.

Uri doesn't even ask if I'm okay. He just looks into the mirror and tells me I don't understand.

Or rather, he uses a line from Act 2, Scene 4 to convey the idea that Icarus doesn't understand, though I understand it to mean that Uri doesn't, given the context. The context being that he is not on the stage and I in the audience, but both of us are here in the duplex, our shared home.

He goes upstairs. I go into his bathroom and turn the water hot, turn it until it is scalding, and splash some on my face. But when I look up into the mirror, the steam has revealed something written, invisible, on the surface.

The mirror is covered—there must be hundreds of them—in tiny pairs of wings.

53

THE GHOST OF BIRDS: *[Indecipherable.]*

52

I am walking to the local library to learn what more I can about the planets, because something inside me is saying that if I learn more about them, I will learn more about Earth, this town, myself. I used to think that was true of physics and astronomy, but these days I only trust what I can see.

Uri keeps trying to get me to use the internet, but I don't want that digital realm where everything is contingent and elastic. I want something I can touch, my finger running down print pages, the smell of the musk of old books. The sound of my pencil lead scraping against paper as I take notes. Luce has told me that the etymology of the word *Earth* is Germanic and English and all it means is grounded. I am walking to the library and I am remembering when there were birds in the sky and they would wake me up in the morning when I was small, when my father was alive, the way I'd watch them perched on trees and then watch them launch into the sky, the sound of their singing moving farther and farther away from me. Earth means grounded, I thought when Luce told me, and then I got sad for Earth because all the other planets had a narrative, a mythology, a name that corresponded with a god. Earth was only the status of humans—forever bound to the ground.

As I walk up the steps of the library, I hear the bus coming. There is a stop just in front of the library that used to be quite popular— many people getting on, many people getting off—and I remember with great fondness idling briefly there at that stop while I waited for people to run out the front doors, waving one arm, the other full of books. I would laugh and yell out, Hello there!, and wave them onto the bus. I'd adjust my tie and sweater vest and wait to pull the bus out of park until they were seated, out of breath.

Now I see the bus coming, the bus without a driver. It stops in front of the library and opens its doors and no one enters or exits. Then it closes its doors and leaves. There is an eeriness to its autonomy that I can't quite put my finger on. It must have to do with the way it follows its orbit around town. When I drove the bus, that looping route felt meaningful, a choice. I could have made a left turn instead of a right—I could have mistakenly taken a wrong way or found a new course when the roads were being worked on. But now, watching the humanless bus navigate that same route, I see the beast as only mechanics, its route locked in, sure as my father's notion that we are living in an imitation world, bound to an already established order.

Inside it is chilly. I hug my oversized sweater a bit tighter around my core.

The library used to be the old firehouse. The walls were tall enough for the fire engines to park, so the shelves of stacks run far up and we have ladders to get the books at the top. Once, a bird got stuck up there and made a nest and then laid eggs and the eggs hatched and for several months you could hear the sound of the baby birds chirping. Then one day the nest was empty. Somehow they'd all escaped.

At a battered wood table, I dig up facts about the planets. I learn that Mercury and Venus—for what reason we do not know—have no moons, that Jupiter's red spot is actually a storm that has been ongoing for over three hundred years, that Uranus has the coldest temperature recorded of any planet. I learn that a day on our moon is just about thirty days here on Earth.

As I am making a note about the fact that the sunsets on Mars are blue, I suddenly hear shouting outside. I look out the huge bay windows and see it's a group of the MAYBE people, and they are shouting, "Neptune!" Everyone in the library goes outside, and when we do, we see them hugging and jumping and a few dancing with each other and a few dancing alone, and others are gathering, running toward those yelling, "Neptune!" I walk over to them, to the MAYBE people, and there it is—Neptune's cement block, half buried by the earth which has swallowed it up and it's been cracked on its left side by a tree root, but it is in fact Neptune. I watch the MAYBE people gather and rejoice and I think about Neptune: the god of fresh water, right here at the library along the town's creek.

Uri says that in really good storytelling, nothing ever ends or dies—rather, everything is merely transformed. Sulien says the same thing about nature. I watch the MAYBE people rejoice together, the MAYBE people who were once NO people and YES people, people who disagreed about everything and gathered weekly to disseminate that disagreement. I am thinking how this strange event of learning our town contains the whole solar system has brought them together and I am wondering what will happen when all the planets have been found. Will they go back to YES and NO people, or have we reached a new era, the era of MAYBE? Will the MAYBE people raise their own children as MAYBE people and will this mean the end of nostalgia for some divisive past and the beginning of something united and collective and new? I see a formerly NO person hug a formerly YES person and in my heart, a beat skips.

Transformation, I think, and then I look up at the sky. I look up to the sky—I behold it—and it is a beautiful day and it looks like we're going to get weather.

51

There is a globe that Luce has given me that is flawed in that it repeats itself along the prime meridian. One half of the globe is the same as the other half of the globe. All of North and South America are missing.

It was jarring the first time I saw it. There was nowhere I could point to on the map that was where I was.

Luce showed it to me when I was very little, when my father was still alive. It gave me chills, so she hid it for a long time.

But the night I told her that the triplets' parents had been killed and I was going to become their legal guardian, I asked if I could see it. She brought it over and I turned it again and again with my finger, spun it over and over while Luce smoked her cigarettes.

"If you could take half of your life and repeat it, which half would you take?" I asked her, watching half the continents blur into themselves again and again.

"The last half," she said.

"Really? I thought for sure you'd say the first."

"The last half because then I get all of it, really. The memories, I mean." She stopped the globe from spinning and asked if she could put her hand on my stomach, to which I said yes.

She had never done this before, had tried to treat the surrogacy as though it was a kind of temporary ailment. She'd ask about my health, if I needed anything. That was about it. She never said what she thought about this choice, the only choice in my mind as to how to become a radio astronomer.

"It's like another kind of globe, huh?" I told her, and she smiled and hung her head. Then I said, "There's a whole world in there."

The next day a man called me, the brother of the woman who was killed. He said he was in mourning and he'd just taken the buy-out from his insurance agency, where he'd been working for thirty years. He said he wanted to help me with the situation, and also that he was writing a play.

He said his name was Uri.

50

LUCE: You know, I was never a triplet, but once I was a twin.

ONE OF THE TRIPLETS: When was that?

LUCE: A long time ago, for a while, I had a brother. He was my twin.

ANOTHER OF THE TRIPLETS: What happened to him?

LUCE: He died.

A THIRD OF THE TRIPLETS: Stars die.

LUCE: How do you know about stars?

ONE OF THE TRIPLETS: Sulien.

LUCE: Stars do die.

ANOTHER OF THE TRIPLETS: When big stars die, they become black holes.

LUCE: Did Sulien tell you that, too?

A THIRD OF THE TRIPLETS: Was your brother a big star?

LUCE: He sure was.

ONE OF THE TRIPLETS: Now your brother is a black hole.

LUCE: *[Crouching down to their level.]* Yes, he is. A big hole in the center of my universe, sucking out the light. *[Beat.]* Now let's go visit the horned lark nest.

49

We are on the porch of our duplex drinking beer and Uri is telling me that a performance is an ephemeral thing, that it doesn't exist the way a print book might. "What do you mean, ephemeral?" I ask, and he says that the performance, it just sort of dissipates into time and space.

"But you just go right back and do the same play the next month," I tell him.

"I'm not talking about the play, I'm talking about the performance," he says. I nod him to go on, but he waits there, presumably to let whatever he said sink in and whatever he's about to say gain meaning. He wants me to understand something. He wants me to listen and in my listening he wants me to know.

"What happens on the stage—it can't be recorded, can't be kept. It's not like one of your tapes that can be rewound over and over indefinitely. The moment it is—that is the very moment it disappears."

I think about the tapes of space and birds and on the one hand, he's right—it is a record. I can replay it and I do.

But then I think that if Uri is right, if what he does is ephemeral and lost as soon as it unfolds, then isn't it more like life? Isn't that more akin to the way time unfolds, or how we experience it? Something so similar to life, so mimetic, reflective of the physical, tangible world, that its power as an artform is just that: it collapses the difference between what is fabrication and what is real.

Uri watches me think and then when he sees that I see him watching, he quickly looks away.

"Is there something you're not telling me, Uri?" I ask him then.

"Yes," he says, and his face grows bright red. Then he shakes his head quickly and wiggles his wings. "No," he says.

"I'll take that as a maybe," I say, and Uri looks terribly disheveled. He doesn't look himself. "I'm here whenever you're ready to talk," I tell him, and I down the rest of my beer and pat him on his wings.

48

There is a sign in my grandfathers' workshop that says this: 180 degrees is half a circle, but also a line.

47

That Saturday at The Demonstration, there are just three people— one NO person, one YES person, and me.

"This isn't shaping up to be much of a demonstration," the NO person says.

"I don't know that we can even make this happen," the YES person says.

"Well," the NO person says, gesturing toward me, "she certainly can't demonstrate for you. It wouldn't make the numbers fair."

"I don't think she should demonstrate for you," the YES person says. "That wouldn't make any sense at all."

They both look at me. "What should we do?"

"This might sound strange," I tell them, "but I have three ice cream sandwiches here in my soft cooler that I was saving for the triplets when The Demonstration was done. I think what we should do is eat them." They consult each other and nod and so we sit on the ground in a circle and we take off the paper and start to eat them and talk.

We talk mostly about how I can't decide if I am a NO or a YES person. They ask me what my parents were, and I respond that I don't really think that matters, since we each have to forge our own path. They ask me if I am a MAYBE person and I tell them that I've thought about that, thought really hard, but I don't think I'm that either. The trouble is, I try to explain, that for each situation or event that crops up in my life, I find myself sometimes feeling like I align with the NO folks and other times like I align with the YES. Still other moments feel firmly MAYBE and others like I don't lean any direction at all.

The NO person licks his thumb where some ice cream has melted. "It's rare, but some people don't decide," he says.

"True," the YES person says, and bites from the bottom of her ice cream sandwich, where it's leaking. "It's rare, but it does, every once in a blue moon, happen."

"I feel like that right there is the trouble," I say. "I don't feel all that alone. I mean," I say, "I feel like there should probably be more people, more people out there who might not be always one kind of person or the other."

There is a silence and we are all looking at each other and it feels like a new kind of energy has emerged between us.

Then the NO person speaks: "Well, I mean, sometimes. Okay, or rather, once—" the NO person says, "so I'll admit that once, just once I did think about going for YES."

"Really?" the YES person says, putting the rest of her sandwich down on the hot asphalt of the parking lot. "Because once—okay, I would say twice, definitely two times, maybe three—I thought about potentially—well, I considered, in a hypothetical way, the possibilities of NO," she said.

"Actually, it was three times for me, considering YES," the NO person says. "Three to five. No more than seven."

"To tell you the truth," the YES person says, "when I'm struggling to go to sleep at night, what I think about is NO. I think about all the ways of NO and how I might fit into those ways."

Something is happening, and it is happening not to me but before me. It feels like I'm watching one of Uri's plays.

"Are you both saying that you aren't firmly YES and NO? But also, neither of you are MAYBE?" I ask. "You don't have to answer that—I'm not pressuring you—it's just that it might help me figure out how I'm going to decide."

"I don't quite know what it means," the YES person says.

"Nor do I," the NO person says.

We sit there, our silence filled with the passing cars instead of the sound of birds, until the designated time at which The Demonstration—if there had been a demonstration—would have concluded.

46

ONE OF THE TRIPLETS: Girl.
ANOTHER OF THE TRIPLETS: Bad.
THE THIRD OF THE TRIPLETS: Curse.
THE TRIPLETS (ALTOGETHER):   Bird.
ONE OF THE TRIPLETS: Bird.
ANOTHER OF THE TRIPLETS: Girl.
THE THIRD OF THE TRIPLETS: Bad.
THE TRIPLETS (ALTOGETHER):   Curse.
ONE OF THE TRIPLETS: Bird.

ANOTHER OF THE TRIPLETS: Curse.

THE THIRD OF THE TRIPLETS: Bad.

THE TRIPLETS (ALTOGETHER):   Girl.

HER: *[Muffled, through the door.]* Please go to sleep.

45

The night Luce finds Pluto, I am late in getting home, having spent the whole day helping Sulien with the star house. She has been keeping her eyes down now and then, as everyone has, trying to spot the planets lodged in the ground. The trick, of course, is that everyone had forgotten about the planet demoted at the turn of the millennium, so no one was looking for it.

That evening Luce asks if I want to take a walk, and I agree and we set off. I'm not sure where we're going, but I let Luce lead and soon I find us walking along the perimeter of our town. Luce walks with a limp, and I can hear her breathe in with a jerk now and then, holding inside her a very ancient kind of pain. It may have to do with my father, the way that she's no longer a twin.

Just as we've gotten as far as the town will allow—the furthest point from the duplex within the town limits—just as I'm about to tell her I'm freezing and we should head back, she knocks her steel-toe boot three times on the ground and I look and there is Pluto. Pluto, the god of the underworld, here next to the town's graveyard. And also, this confirms it: the contours of our town are precisely overlaid with that of the dimensions of the solar system, give or take some fuzziness at the border. But borders as a rule are fuzzy, and in this case I equate that fuzziness with the vague limits of the Kuiper belt.

I ask her to tell me more about the imitation world my father felt we are a part of. She looks at me with raised eyebrows.

"I don't believe it, but it calms me to hear you say it," I say. "Like a fairy tale."

She sighs and asks me if I have a light.

Luce says that my father believed we were all part of a very great fabricated reality, that we have been placed here strategically, as part of a way of knowing what kind of patterns humans will discover and what kind of patterns humans will invent. Then, as if to illustrate this point, she uses the tip of her steel-toed boot to make a circle in the soil and then she makes shapes inside the circle that look like portions of continents. She tells me that my father believed some other cognition was watching us and our fabricated reality. It would keep watching us until it learned what it needed to know, and then—then it would end things abruptly. Everything would rush toward a single point that he called The Beautiful End. It would be like those old analogue television sets turning off. The way when you flipped the switch, the light and sound would bend until it disappeared into the vortex at the center of the screen. Then she takes her shoe and runs it over the world slowly until the soil is just a big smear.

I can't help thinking that The Beautiful End, the old TV turning off—it sounds precisely like what happens at the center of a black hole.

"He knew he was made of flesh and blood and bone," she says, and I can't help looking out over the graveyard, "a creature bound to the laws of entropy, but he believed he was an organic being caught in an artificial construction. Sort of like an ant farm—the ants themselves are real, but the terrain they navigate is false. We build it just to watch."

She goes on to explain that he thought we all believe we have agency because it is simpler that way, to believe that we are the engineers of our own happiness and sorrow. But my father believed that the laws of the world were the work of some cognition beyond our understanding.

"But doesn't that mean we don't have control over our choices? Doesn't that mean that all of the cruelty of which we are capable is

not human-made and human-induced—that it's all unfolding because of some other force?" I ask. "To me, that feels like a cop-out."

"Your father would have pointed out that you're talking about
the ants, there," Luce says. "Humans aren't responsible for the way
the ants behave, who they harm, who they love, how they build and
destroy their own farm. Humans are only responsible for construct-
ing the environment and letting the ants do what they will."

I can't believe how much I disagree with this theory of my father's. It's actually a bit jarring, disagreeing with him this much. I
don't think I've ever felt so certain he was wrong.

But I also know the ways his brain filled in the blanks of logic
with feeling and desire, the ways his sense of what was fact and what
was fiction would blur and overlap, intersect. I fear because I know
this is a trait that he has passed to me, this way of privileging feeling
over reason.

"You know better than he did," she says, "that things have a beginning." And I do know, because it was radio astronomy that led us
to the theory of the Big Bang. "But I've said enough."

"No—I'm listening. I'm trying to listen. I know you aren't trying
to convince me, I know that. I just want to hear what he thought. He
never spoke about this."

She kicks one shoe on the sole of the other and vice versa, runs
her hand over her shaved head. "Wish your grandfathers were here,"
she says. I don't say anything then.

"I can see that all this unsettles you," she says, and it does. It
actually shakes the core of me, feels the way you feel when you've
read a horror story and it haunts you and in order to calm your mind
you tell yourself it's fake, only to learn later it's actually based on a
story that's true. "He made you a tape once, on your tenth birthday.
Explained all of this to you. I think it was on one of the bird tapes.
Wish we knew where that tape went."

She fingers the notch on the top of her ear, shakes her head.

She drops her cigarette and crushes it, leans down and picks the

butt up. "He believed there was an order out there, and everyone—
you and I and he—we were all falling into it. If he were here now,
he would say that our whole life is a kind of order we're falling into
slowly, one day at a time," she says, and puts the spent butt in her
handkerchief and shoves it in her pocket.

"It's important to know," she says, and she looks me in the eye,
pauses. "What I want you to know is that some truths are uncomfortable. But he preferred to know them, rather than bury his head
in the sand."

"But Luce," I say then, "are we talking about our truths? Or just
his?"

She looks up at the sky, then down at her feet. She looks at the
cemetery around her. "There is more than one reality," she says, and I
can't help thinking she sounds like Sulien. "Each of us has to find our
own and then work through how that reality fits in with others' realities—shared and independent. Part of all of this," she says, absently
waving her hand perhaps to signify life or perhaps to indicate death,
"part of all this is finding your route, one that leads you safely through
both your own reality and the realities you share. If you're lucky, you
find that route, difficult as it may be. Sometimes it happens relatively
early. Sometimes it takes one's whole life. For others, though…" She
pauses for a moment. "Sometimes others don't find it at all."

I feel the blood pulsing in my veins. What she is saying reminds
me that time moves at a different rate for humans than for birds.

I feel my face flush. I feel my heart hurt.

I nod to her and she nods back. "Since we're here?" she says, and
we walk over to my father's memorial. It's a bench we made him, with
his name on it, and the years he spent on the crust of the Earth. Then
we walk the perimeter of our town, quietly. We are reflecting. I am
thinking that Luce is thinking her twin brother thought this was all
a construction, an illusion. I wonder for a moment what that does to
the idea of plot, to the idea of cause-and-effect.

For me, I am thinking about my father and the way that he lives on, shadow-like, in Luce's face. In the way she walks, in the shape of her fingernail beds. In her voice and in the cowlick above her left eye. My father was composed of these same parts, but separately, and I watch Luce age and I wonder what it would be like for my father. What their friendship would have been like, in what unique ways their siblinghood would have taken shape in these later years. I want to believe that Luce is what is left of my father, but I know better than that. Luce is her own man, and my father is gone. Luce could have left me, and she didn't.

We walk and walk—we are walking from the farthest point within the town limits to the place that I call home, we are walking the full span of the solar system. I hug my oversized sweater around me closer. When we get home I realize suddenly, a bit sadly, that I didn't even look up once to see if I could spot a star which means, to my sorrow, I am growing used to the world without them.

"Luce?" I say, when I split off to head toward the duplex and she keeps going north to get to her house.

"Yep," she says.

"You found Pluto," I tell her and smile.

She grunts. "It's easy to find something no one else is looking for," she says.

I nod a goodnight to her, and she nods right back. Then I go inside and shake Uri from his sleep on my couch and he hugs me, barely awake, and heads out my front door, and a fraction of a second later I hear him heading in his front door, then upstairs to his room.

I sit in the rocker of the triplets' room and listen to the sounds of space, watch the slow rise and fall of three tiny chests as the bodies of the triplets conduct their breathing.

I pull the sleeves of my sweater over my hands, hug my legs with my arms, and use the force of my form to make the chair rock.

I think: I am real.

I think: Luce is wrong. We are not just words. And my father is wrong. This isn't a simulation.

This is real. All of this is real.
I exist and we are here and this is now and I—
I am real.

44

HER TWO-WAY RADIO: *[Static.]*

43

Once, when we were leaving the library on an especially hot summer day, when we exited the building and the heat consumed us immediately, the chill of the library's air conditioning making a stark and visceral line between inside and outside—as we were walking to the bus stop to get a ride back to town, The Only Person I've Ever Loved and I came upon an egg on the sidewalk.

The shell was a light yellow with specks of dark brown. We could not see an opening.

"It's got to be dead," I said.

"Must have rolled out of the nest or something," she replied.

We stood there watching it for a while before I heard the bus breaking around the block and told her we needed to get to the stop or it'd pass us up.

Very lightly, she pushed the egg with her finger. Suddenly we could see it—the hole that had been hidden by the way the egg sat.

She picked it up, relief saturating her body, and placed it on her palm. I told her that was really unsanitary, and she shrugged. The hole was small, but it didn't strike us as strange then. What we thought was that the bird was free.

I only learned much later, after the birds were gone, that what likely happened is that a predator had gotten to it, made the hole, and sucked the soft body of the baby bird from the shell it called home.

42

I've tucked the triplets in but I'm still in their room, listening to the sounds of space. I'm in their room rocking in my father's rocking chair, thinking of what Uri said, and what he didn't say.

I think of the people whom I love and how they operate in this strange yet familiar world. Luce reads to the triplets and begrudgingly completes her shifts at The Farm, Sulien tends the giant nests and builds the star house, Uri performs his play and wears his wings. The Conglomerates conglomerate until all corporations become, essentially, one. The bus with no driver keeps making its loop, and the road that goes nowhere dead ends.

I think of when Uri told me the end of the play was once called The Catastrophe. But life is not a play, as far as I believe. We can avoid the last act. We are in The Crisis, but it need not become The Catastrophe.

At The Demonstration, I used to ask the NO people when I was on their side and ask the YES people when I chose theirs—did they also feel this ongoing, exponential dread? Did they also experience this dual and paradoxical feeling of being at once utterly powerless to entrenched patterns and also totally capable of revolution? But both sides would remind me—in their own way, using the particular rhetoric of YES and the very different rhetoric of NO—that, essentially, I can't change the world.

Which is true, but also, I always thought that believing you could was the first step. Knowing you couldn't was obvious, but making believe you could—that is how the change began. By tricking yourself into believing you were the narrator of your own story and because of that, you could initiate change—to the setting and the conflict and the end.

41

The night after Luce finds Pluto, as I am trying to fall asleep, I hear Uri on the wall—three knocks. Just as I'm reaching up to knock back, he does it again, three times, but slower, with more space in between, and then again three times, back to the original pace.

This is not our sign—our sign is three knocks by one of us, then three knocks in response, and then we are free to enter the front door of the other. This is different. He keeps doing it over and over, and then I realize that it's Morse code he's knocking. He's knocking to me Morse code for SOS.

It is not a summons. It's a lament.

To show him that he's not alone, I knock back. Save our ship, save our ship, save our ship.

Fantasy is dangerous, my father used to say. Don't be deceived by castles in the air.

I knock to him and he knocks back and we do this for a while and then he stops and soon after I hear his gentle snoring. On the other side of my room the star charts are rolled up and I get out of bed and unroll them. I take thumb tacks and stand on my bed and post the charts on the ceiling. I stare at the stars and listen to Uri snore and imagine the sounds of the deepest part of the ocean until I fall asleep.

40

That Saturday I make my way to The Demonstration. But when I arrive, not a single person is there. I sit on the edge of the parking lot, waiting for someone else to come, but no one does.

I have a whole hour without the triplets, so I walk to Luce's house and sit in her front yard among the flawed globes. There are desk globes and wall globes and floor globes, and they are all stuck in the ground with giant metal poles at various heights. Some are newer, the papier-mâché leaving a thin layer of gloss, and others are so old and weathered there is only the echo of Earth's crust left on an otherwise light blue roundness.

I sit there in the yard and I wonder if the old town feud is over. And if it is, what part have I played in it, even as I myself am the great traitor, the one who can't decide.

Then I hear it—the bus with no driver—coming up the road.

I want to hate it, but how can I? It is the same as me, an autonomous vehicle trying to navigate all the silly and sad obstacles of this life in order to do what it does best. We are the same, I think, watching the bus drive by. Two machines following the paths we inherited. I let the bus pass, and when it does, I nod to it in understanding.

39

The day of the eclipse I woke to a cardinal knocking twice on my window over and over again as if to say this is the day you've been waiting for. It has arrived at last. Come and meet it.

38

Sulien and I are sitting in the nest of the American robin, looking up at the light-polluted sky. I can hear his breathing and feel the warmth of it near me, and I think of this act of breathing—how necessary, how fundamentally crucial—and how it is a little bit like a minor miracle that this ongoing event happens all the time, happens repeatedly without us knowing, but is also the source of how and why we continue to persevere. It is kind of like weather, ongoing to the point of being invisible. It's only when we get scope and scale, when we get distance, that we can assess the climate.

I remember that first breath, the three first breaths of the triplets who exited my body and in turn entered the world, how for a moment my body was a vessel inside a larger world and then, in one bright instant, it suddenly wasn't. They were free of me. I imagine it's the same sensation a bird has when they look back at their shell, that border between one kind of home and another.

The triplets and those first three breaths are on my mind. I look at Sulien and he looks at me and he says, "Look." Sulien says, "See." And I look up, toward the sky.

The one thing most people know about the stars is that everything we see has already happened. The night sky is a kind of trace, because light takes time, and for the light from the stars and planets to reach our eyes—back when the stars and planets did reach our eyes—a great deal of time has unfolded. And while I've known this for a long time, it is only now that I think of Uri telling me that a play is always performed in present tense and I realize the trace of the light in the sky means something else, also: that when we look up, we can never see now.

Sulien explains that in order to do the star house the way he wants—with the removeable ceilings so that as each season changes, he can take out the old season's orientation of the night sky and substitute the new one—we've got a few more skies to build.

Then Sulien asks me a question: he asks me the distance between Saturn and us here on Earth.

"In millions of kilometers, Astronomical units, or time?" I ask him, and I hear him say that he'd like to know the distance in time.

"The distance," I say, "between Saturn and Earth," I say, grateful that I have the answer, "is 1.18 light hours. That means if we could see Saturn in the sky, what we would see is Saturn 1.18 hours ago."

"What about Mercury?" he asks.

"Mercury? That's 5.18 light minutes, which means the Mercury we'd see—if we could see it, if there wasn't smog and light pollution blocking the way—would be Mercury 5.18 minutes ago."

Then Sulien asks me all the other planets. What is their distance from us?

My work in this world is to listen. It is what I do most, though not best, and in that regard, many of those closest to me share what it is they believe, what it is they know. Luce tells me about globe creation and revision. Uri tells me about writing plays. Sulien tells me about the birds, and the triplets inform me of black holes. The NO people tell me of their miseries, the YES of their triumphs. The folks on the bus used to tell me beautiful stories that would pause when they got off the bus at their stop and then start back up the next time they rode, the next day, the next week—stories that would stretch for months, for years. The Only Person I've Ever Loved told me all her secrets and I've kept a tight hold on them ever since.

It is rare, I realize then, that I am able to share with others the knowledge I have. I studied for that test for years, failed it five times, and yet, I have never shared that information, the insight I hoarded inside me, with anyone else. And now that I've stopped studying, now that I've grown familiar with my failure—now that I've given myself a pass to fail—I barely remember any of what I was studying, can't recall much at all.

But what I do know and can recall is this:

Venus is 2.3 light minutes from Earth. The triplets were born on a Thursday. The Only Person I've Ever Loved bites her fingernails. Once, long ago, when she was still a child, no one was watching Luce when she took a knife off the counter and took off the top of her ear.

Mars is 4.35 light minutes from Earth. To make a globe, you build the world one strip at a time. The piping plover would pretend to be injured to distract an enemy from its young. The Big Bang was the first and only cause, and its effect has been everything after.

My grandfathers—my father's fathers—were deeply, madly, passionately in love. Sulien's partner was lost in a way similar to my father. Luce has over 150 globes in her yard. My first day driving the bus was the first day in my life that I felt truly proud of myself. Jupiter is 34.95 light minutes from Earth.

The Crisis is filling my blood with dread. The eclipse came on a Monday. The word *disaster* comes from the Latin for "an ill-starred event." Sulien once told me that I needed to speak up more and I've been trying hard to do so ever since. The Only Person I've Ever Loved is exactly six months older than me. When you talk to them, really dig deep into what they care about and how they understand, what they actually believe, there is virtually no difference between the worldviews of the NO people and the YES people.

Uranus is 2.52 light hours from Earth. The male albatross spent 95% of its life over the open ocean. No one alive knows who was born first, Luce or my father. The triplets all have the same birthmark under the nipple of their right breast. I discovered a single gray hair at the crown of the head of The Only Person I've Ever Loved when we were fifteen and I never told her. The girl in Girl in Glass Vessel doesn't know she's inside a glass vessel. Crows could remember human faces that had in some way wronged them. Neptune is 4.03 light hours from Earth.

The Only Person I've Ever Loved once built me a bird's nest the size of my hand, and when she gave it to me, she told me she'd built me a home and to get inside it.

If a human being lived precisely one hundred years and transposed their life over the lifespan of the planet, people would have only walked Earth for the last nine hours before death.

I am in the middle of The Crisis.

The Catastrophe can be avoided.

The Catastrophe doesn't have to come.

The only bird that could fly backward was the hummingbird.

Pluto is 4.6 light hours from Earth.

37

I have one memory of my grandfathers, though I do not know if it is a real memory or a story I have been told so many times that it has become entangled in my brain and stored there as having happened.

It is a day when I am small and Luce and my father are not with us and I am being watched by Grandad and PaPa. Tornadoes line the horizon. We are heading to the root cellar and PaPa lifts me up. Grandad asks where we are going and PaPa says we'll be right back. I can see Grandad's face grow smaller and smaller as PaPa carries me away and outside.

PaPa sets me down in the yard filled with globes. The sky is a vivid green, like it wants to be the earth or the ocean. PaPa kneels down next to me. He tells me to listen. The sound is extraordinary. I had not realized the sky could be so loud. The wind pushes and pulls in all directions. The clouds move faster than I can follow, sweeping from the sky to the horizon. It feels like everything that is familiar to me—the yard of my grandfathers, the trees I climbed, the garden from which I helped to gather our meals—was covered in a strange veil.

In my memory that is perhaps not a real memory, this is the story I tell myself unfolded that day. And in my telling, this is the moment that I come to understand that the world crafts its own cadence. It is the clouds that help me know this, the clouds that teach me the tender beat that lives beneath all things.

Suddenly, in the memory-story, Grandad appears, yelling over the rush of the wind, Please come inside. Now. PaPa looks at me to make sure he has conveyed what he hoped. I signal that he has by lifting my arms so he can pick me up.

Then the three of us go into the basement and wrap in blankets. We listen for the radio to announce that all is clear.

36

SULIEN: The chickadee had the most sophisticated communication system of any land animal. Of any land animal! *[Beat.]* We tried and tried for years, but in the end, we never cracked its code.

HER: Was there really a code?

SULIEN: It feels nice to believe there was. But that might be because I am human and seek order in all things.

HER: What could the code have meant?

SULIEN: Probably they were sharing all the secrets of the world— singing them into our ears, day and night, over and over—and we chose not to listen.

35

URI: *[Knocking on the wall, unaware that she is not on the other side.]*
··· — — — ···

34

I am knocking on Luce's front door and I am not getting a response. I am knocking and knocking and then I give up and sit on the porch and adjust the handheld two-way radio in the front pocket of my overalls.

That is when I hear a sound coming from the garage around the back of the house. The sound is a human humming.

I walk around the back and there is Luce, in the garage, mixing a huge vat of something that looks like thick milk with a massive wooden spoon. On the long worktable behind her there are three globes that I have never seen before, three globes that look old but well-kept, that—from what I can tell—have never been in this garage.

She looks up from her work but doesn't miss a beat, keeps stirring and humming and nods a hello.

I stand there for a few minutes, watching her work, and then I decide to sit down, settle into one of the benches. On the seat of the bench to my left, there are the names of Grandad and PaPa seared into the wood, a plus sign between them, and then beneath that in a beautiful, haunting font the word *forever*.

I watch Luce for a long while, my knees pulled up underneath me, my chin resting on them, the two-way radio's dull static a lovely background to Luce's humming.

Finally, she speaks. "A few folks—not your generation, but older, my generation and earlier—over the years, a few folks have asked me to revise their globes. I've always told them no. But today," she says, and she lifts the spoon high to test the serum's viscosity, "today I put in my two weeks at The Farm and then called each of them up and said I'd do it."

She nods to the worktable behind her and the three globes lined up on top.

"But then," she says, and she shakes her head and smiles at the ground. "Come here."

We walk together from the garage around to the house's back entrance. As soon as she opens the door, I see it right away—the kitchen table is full of globes. And the kitchen floor, globes stacked up on the chairs and counters. Globes leading into the living area, and stacked up there, too.

"Seems word got around quickly," she says. "And those are just the revisions. The orders for new globes are here." She lifts up a stack of papers and presses them to my chest. I flip through and read the details about the requested size and color scheme, political or physical, what language.

"The older folks in town want new ones for your generation—the young adults—and the younger generations, too."

"Luce," I say, and just as I say it, I look at the table and see a globe with a piece of tape on the base and on the tape is the name *Sulien*. I spin it gently with my thumb. "This is incredible. Who knew?" I smile despite myself. This is something I didn't see coming, something my déjà vu had not prepared me for, and I am grateful that the world is still willing to let itself surprise me. "You up for the challenge?"

I have never seen Luce get choked up, not even at my father's funeral. I decide it must be the glue making her eyes go glossy.

And then she says it, her mantra: "Feels wrong not to try."

33

Sulien has asked if I want to do a test run. "Get inside," he says, and I slip into the completed star house.

To avoid more cracks that would let light in, he has created ladder-like steps on the outside and on the inside of one wall. I climb up the ladder outside and then flip my leg over the wall and climb down the ladder on the other side until I'm inside.

The star house is of a decent size. Before he shifts the lid closed, he tells me to move around. "Move around," he says. "It's the opposite of a planetarium where you sit still and the stars move. Here it's the stars that stay static—you have to walk around." Then he pulls the ceiling over me.

I look up above me and my breath catches in my throat. They're so bright—perfect holes of different sizes, with an otherworldly shimmer. A memory comes fighting through, trying to return, and I catalog the way the stars are organized. I see this huge cup, a kind of ladle created from the way the stars shape themselves, or rather, created from the way my mind shapes the stars. Something in my mind clicks into place, which is really just recall meeting language, and I mouth silently: The Big Dipper.

I hear Sulien's voice then. "How's it looking?"

That is when something moves from the hazy part of my mind, tucked far in the back, and becomes a sharp point right at the front of my forehead almost instantly. It is a memory of my father hoisting me up and then sitting me on the back of his neck, pointing to the shapes the night's lights formed.

Sulien's voice again asks what I see.

"I see a sliver of light in the northwest corner that we'll need to plug up. But I also see the sky at night, like when I was a child. It's fantastic. Almost real."

"Stay in there a minute," he tells me. I walk around and look up, and all these memories from when we could see the stars come from their misty space in my mind. And I think, how much of the world is hidden back there in the empty folds of my brain, never to be recalled again? And I think: how much of what is not recalled are beautiful memories lost, and how much of it is ugly memories that I'm better off without?

The stars are bright, or rather the sun posing as the stars, the day disguised as the night, and this feels true. This feels right.

"How much time does it take for the Sun's light to reach Earth?" Sulien asks me.

And I say, "Eight light minutes."

The eclipse is over, and The Crisis is here, and what is time, I think, and also I think of the bags beneath Luce's eyes and the weight of a single triplet's hand in the palm of my own.

Then Sulien shifts the lid and the fantasy is broken. It is just me in a box and Sulien smiling down on me from his foothold on the ladder, reaching his hand out to help a fellow person up.

That fellow person being me.

32

THE GHOST OF BIRDS: *[Indecipherable.]*

31

"Did you ever get to see a murmuration of starlings?" I ask Sulien.

"Of course. You?"

"Not in real life. Only on the internet," I say.

"Isn't that real life?"

"Not according to Uri."

"Actually, Uri told me that there is no real life, that we are always, to some extent, in a state of performance. That the social realm is really just a stage, and there's no essential you or me, it's all just different degrees of show."

"Uri's not doing well lately," I say, and Sulien looks at me for a moment and I look back, look deep into his eyes and something happens there, a connection, a desire to want to talk about our shared sorrows, but neither of us will break the silence and speak.

So I go on. "It's just amazing to me how they moved, almost like water. How were they able to flock together like that? Was there a leader guiding them?"

"Nope," Sulien says, as we lift this portion of the ceiling. When we get it vertical, we very gently angle it downward until it's horizonal, covering the star house top. "No leader. It was all a coordinated, collective effort," he says. "Each bird followed the seven birds closest to it."

"What do you mean?" I ask.

"Instead of focusing on the movement of the whole flock, each bird would try to make their moves sync with its seven neighbor birds. That's why it looks like water ebbing and flowing in the sky. Because there's a delay between each bird following its closest seven."

I am holding one portion of the night sky and I am doing the math: Sulien, Uri, Luce. The triplets. The Only Person I've Ever Loved.

And, in the middle, trying to follow them all: me.

30

URI: I've been having terrible thoughts.

LUCE: You know better than that.

URI: I can't stop it.

LUCE: *[Leaning behind him to adjust his wings.]* You're going to be okay. We're—all of us—going to be okay.

URI: Cause and effect.

LUCE: I guess, Uri. But have you noticed that it's the effect you see first? You see the effect and then, only after, do you look for the cause. So it's sort of the other way around.

URI: The king died, and then the queen died of grief.

LUCE: You are always saying that. But what I find myself wondering is: what killed the king?

29

"What killed the king?" Luce asks me, and I look up from the laundry, startled. I am taking it down from the line that runs from the front of our porch to the pole in the center of our tiny front yard. Luce is collecting the pins and asking me what killed the king. And who gave birth to the king and also, while we're at it, the queen, and what sorrow preceded their parents' parents and was there ever a time when there wasn't a monarchy, when the king and queen as concepts didn't exist?

"The problem with Uri's theory of cause and effect," Luce says, "is that it just keeps tracking back. How can you call the king's death the cause of the queen's when it was really their falling in love that caused her death, his being born, his parents' parents meeting, the formation of the whole damn kingdom? You track back far enough and everything loses its cause."

"But that seems dangerous," I tell her, "thinking that the world is just effects. Seems like thinking that way means no one should be held accountable."

And she says: "Maybe. But I also wonder if it's more dangerous to imagine that every effect has a singular, simple beginning."

We finish with the laundry and she asks me about The Demonstration and I tell her, as I often do, that there were two sides and I was on one of them, though I realize that's not really true anymore. And she laughs and offers me a cigarette and I refuse because, I tell her, I have decided to stop smoking, and she gives me a look that might possibly mean she's proud.

Then I say, "I'm worried about Uri. He's getting really bad."

"We all have to figure out how to travel the path of moderation," she says, and stares at me hard.

"I know, but Luce—"

"I hear you," she says. "I know." She lights a cigarette. "By the way. It comes from the Middle English and Greek for study and the Anglo-French for real or true."

"What does?" I ask her. The static from my two-way radio amplifies a bit when I stand.

"*Etymology*," she says. "It's amazing what escapes our line of vision when it's right under our nose."

28

That first phone conversation I'd had with Uri all those years ago, years that seem like decades to me but also feel like they unfolded just yesterday—in that first phone conversation, I asked Uri why insurance.

I'd told him I was dead set on being a radio astronomer, that raising the triplets would cause a delay in that dream, but it would unfold nevertheless. I told him work was important to me, what a person chooses to spend their life doing, training to become, in what ways a person conducts their labor to make the world a slightly less awful place.

"Why insurance?" I asked him.

"Fell into it really," he said. "It was a job and I took it. Then got promoted. Then there was Friday night karaoke, fewer haircuts as I grew it out and began to braid it, the year I read every play by Marlowe and Webster over and over again. Then I failed to fall in love. Once. Three times. The theater's productions had fewer runs, groceries got more expensive, the internet entered each region of what it meant to be a person in the Western world, then The Crisis. Then I arrived at the end like I'd arrived at the beginning, falling into it: my boss knocked on my cubicle wall and they offered me the buyout."

He cleared his throat into the mouth of the phone. "So as far as why insurance? It wasn't my dream. My dream was to write a play."

"Is," I told him, and he was quiet for a moment before he replied. "My dream *is* to write a play."

27

URI: [*Knocking on the wall, in the middle of the night, when she is fast asleep.*] … __ __ __ …

26

After the MAYBE people find Neptune, three weeks pass before it's clear: Earth is missing.

"Neptune was big, a turning point," Sulien is telling me. We are at the American robin nest, taking in the clouds and smog. One strange effect of The Crisis is that everything has more color, though that color, we all know, is laced with grief and guilt, the way you can see the rainbow in a parking lot's puddle of gasoline.

"Though the front is now united, tensions are high. There's an organized pursuit and round-the-day searchers working that orbit hard."

"What will happen if they can't find it?"

"Truthfully? I don't believe it's even there," he says.

"No Earth? Come on. There has to be."

"Oh, I'm sure there is an earth," he says, "but it doesn't resemble what they're looking for."

25

I go to the community center and visit the Bird Wing, but when I look at the wall, all I see is the image of the triplets' drawing. The whole wall is only it and nothing else, the scratchy Vs coming straight at me.

On my long walk home, I find myself wondering if the rest of our contributions are underneath their drawing, or if they were ever there at all.

24

From the beginning, Uri says, and I take a long swig from my beer. He turns around and starts the play over again. And then I'm listening to Act 1, then Act 2, then Act 3. Uri says, "The flight paths of the past, though spectral, frame the future."

From the beginning, Uri says, and I am wondering what got me to this point, what series of cause-and-effect chains have set me on this course. I am trying to remember this morning, or yesterday, but all those days seem to slip into and around each other. I can't quite tell one hour, one day, one year from the next, nor whether they are memories, events I've already lived or if they are the present, the life I'm living in one of many versions of Now. And then I hear Uri say: "Somewhere in the cosmos, Earth's twin reveals our mirror-lives."

From the beginning, Uri says. I could be sitting here for three hours or twelve, two days or ten, possibly a year, maybe my whole life. How old are the triplets, where is my father, when will I tell The Only Person I've Ever Loved that I loved her, why is this town the town that it is. I must have had too much to drink, but when I try to count the number of beers I've had, I'm certain it's only the one in my hand. And then Uri: "Yes, no, no, yes, yes, yes, no, no. Yes, no, yes, yes, no, yes, no—no, yes, no."

From the beginning, Uri says. I think: Luce once explained to me how to build a globe.

And then, I see it out of the corner of my eye and turn to look completely: there it goes, the bus that drives itself.

23

Sound can travel a bit under five miles in a single second. That is how long it takes for my father's voice to enter my ear through the tape player. Of course, it has also taken fourteen years for me to lift this particular tape from its case and press play.

It's a recording of a Western meadowlark, and at the end suddenly I can hear my father's voice cut in: "Hey kiddo, come here. See that? It's—" and then the recording stops.

I had never known his voice had been caught on this tape, or any other. It's his voice, sure as rain, and I catapult back in time to then, my whole form and mind, my whole person lives for a moment in that moment, and it is bitter and it is sweet, for on the same tape live the voices of two gone beings: my father and the birds.

That night, as I'm trying to fall asleep, I pull out the tape player and play the very end. Then I rewind it, play it again. "Hey kiddo, come here. See that? It's—" I hear it once, then four times, fifteen.

"Hey kiddo, come here. See that? It's—"

"Hey kiddo, come here. See that? It's—"

I play it over and over again, but soon it starts to lose its meaning. Like the triplets repeating a word until it is just sound, just a creature expelling something sonic, until there is nothing conveyed or communicated at all.

"Hey kiddo, come here. See that? It's—" I play it one last time and then I let myself wonder for a moment how the sentence ended. I try to uncover what he said next.

22

The MAYBE people keep revolving around the invisible orbits governing this town. The MAYBE people are caught in those orbits.

"It's a revolution," Sulien says, and when I look at him, confused, he points to a long line of people walking in pairs or single file, no one more than three folks wide, circling and circling our town.

I think then of my life long ago, my grandfathers holding my tiny hands as we make circles around the sundial in the center of our town, over and over, collecting good luck. I think of The Only Person I've Ever Loved and I, doing the same thing years later.

"A revolution," he says, and I realize it's true. They will keep revolving around the sundial until they've found Earth, and maybe, hopefully, after.

21

THE GHOST OF BIRDS: *[Indecipherable.]*

20

"Do you want me to go in with you?" I ask them, and all three of the triplets shake their heads.

Sulien and Uri and I each grab one and go up the ladder of the star house. We put them inside the box. Then we climb out.

"You sure you're okay in there?" I ask them, and I hear the trio of their small voices respond with a series of *yeahs*.

Sulien puts the lid down and begins to slide it across the top. When he's halfway, he nods for me to ask them if they're still okay, and when they say again that they are, he slides it the rest of the way.

We are silent then, waiting for them to experience this, waiting for this experience to permeate them. In that time, I begin to feel a deep and penetrating sorrow that I have to give them this instead of the real night sky. But then I think about my déjà vu, that notion that perhaps my dreams have been feeding me my future for the whole of my life, and I think of the triplets and how much of their dreams are right now, on these very nights, feeding them a future that they will come to meet. And maybe in that future, there will be stars.

They are quiet—they have been silent since we closed the star house—but we can hear them walking around, getting a sense of the whole space, seeing the angles differently. We let them stay for ten minutes, then twenty, thirty. When we're coming up on an hour, I ask Sulien to take off the lid. He pulls it off quickly in one long swipe.

I climb the ladder and look in and there are the triplets, lying on the ground: three heads meeting in the center, their legs outstretched, their arms still in the air pointing upward. They are whispering to each other, but what they say I cannot hear, and when I ask them if they want to come out, they say not now or ever.

They stay on the ground and ask to have the night sky put back, and tell me that they never, not ever, not for anything at all—never do they ever want to leave.

19

HER TWO-WAY RADIO: *[Static.]*

18

The day I finally parked the bus and walked home from the depot for the last time, I remember I took the long way home and swung by Saturn to remind myself there are larger things at play than just me and my infinitesimal problems.

We move on. Sulien and I tend the giant nests, keep them ready to be used. Luce continues building and revising the globes for the townsfolk to remember that beyond the limits of this local system lies a much larger community. The MAYBE people orbit, searching for Earth. Uri conducts his play, and every evening after he is done, I can hear him weeping from his side of the duplex.

Tonight, when I hear Uri start, I knock three times on his wall and the crying stops and he knocks back and I enter his duplex and walk up to this room and he falls into me and I catch him. I lead him out to the porch, and Uri lies across me and puts his head in my lap and I stroke his wings very gently, running the length of my fingers down the intricately webbed and networked wire lattice and all the material tucked into it that—altogether—compose his wings.

Uri is telling me that what you need to do is embody the character and suture it to yourself. It is not as if the part is separate from you, he says. But the problem, he is telling me, the problem is that when you've done that, you start to lose any sense of control. The problem, really, is the fall—he knows it's coming every time, feels it en route. He knows each time he performs the play he will be ending himself.

"You mean Icarus," I tell him. "You will be ending Icarus, not yourself," I tell him.

Of course, he tells me using a line from Act 2, Scene 1.

"But Uri," I say, "you've ended the play before the fall. You are actually saving him from that fate each and every time you perform it."

"I thought that's what I was doing," he tells me. "But me and everyone out there—we know the real ending. And it's not just the ending of the story of Icarus. I'm talking about The Crisis. Everyone knows what's coming, even if I choose not to show it to them."

He is breathing really heavily then and he says, suddenly louder, "The trick is trying to forget where everything is leading. It's got to be the one and only time every time I do it. I've got to forget what happens after the play ends, forget about The Catastrophe."

"Did you know," I say, "that in space, freefall doesn't feel like falling at all? It feels like staying perfectly still." His body starts to tremble and shiver, and I can hear him gasping for breath as he weeps.

We are silent for a while. I let him do the work his body and his mind needs to do, which is to move through the sorrow with a good balance of tears and time. This is work I came to understand when I'd care for my father.

Then, when Uri's body is no longer quaking—you have to wait for the body to calm—I speak.

"You know, sometimes," I say, "I can hear myself speaking to myself."

He looks up at me. I stop stroking his wings.

"Sometimes I hear myself telling the story of myself. I don't know who I'm telling it to."

He pulls away from me then, sits up and looks at me head on.

"When I'm telling this story, the story of myself, I hear the way I am creating this cohesive portrait of the person I am, of the things that are happening around me. I can hear that. But the truth is that between the way it feels and the way I tell it, there is a thin space there, a cavity. When I try to translate what I am feeling to language, even if that language is just in my head, something is lost."

He looks at me then like I am on to something, something I don't need to tell him but that I need to tell myself. "What are you saying?"

"That no one—not the narrator or the characters, not the actors or the audience—ever gets access to the real story. You can play the tape back a million times, you can reread the story for eternity, and each time, something will go unheard."

He resumes his spot in my arms. We are quiet for a while.

Then I ask him if he'd like me to wash his wings.

He stands up on the porch that has been his stage and nods his head up and down. "But first," he says, "can you help me molt?"

There is ephemera covering his wings—fabric braided in, pieces from board games, sea glass, a fake bird nest, several business cards, a dozen hair clips, a few pencils, two small spiral notebooks, a menu from a local restaurant, a crown of dead flowers. We dismantle everything, one piece at a time, and when his wings are just the bare wire that Luce crafted for him all those weeks ago, I lead him into his side of the duplex and draw him a bath and undress him except for his wings. I test the water, then lead him into the bath and I wash first his flesh with a cloth lathered with soap and then I wash his wings, still bound to his back. I had forgotten how beautiful the wire was underneath all the decoration. When I soap them up the light gets inside the spaces and they look like a bug's wings, all the colors shifting and morphing from pink to turquoise to yellow. I take swigs from my beer as I'm washing him and I hum these low notes that remind me of the way a mourning dove would sound in the late afternoon, back when there were birds, and Uri closes his eyes. I take the washcloth and lather it with soap and I run the cloth over him, over his pale arms, over his back, watch the way his wrinkled skin sags and pulls and moves like sand. I hum and run the cloth over him and his eyes are closed and it looks like he's going to cry again but then he smiles and starts humming, too. He breaks only to reach for my beer, takes a swig before handing the can to me, and we go back and forth like that, finishing it off, humming the loose memory of some gone species' song.

I am listening to Uri, but as I listen I am also thinking an unshared thought, a thought shared with no one at all—I get the feeling that I am being observed, that someone else hears me, has admission to these thoughts. Like the actors on the stage, but reversed—I'm not trying to forget the audience that lies clearly before me, I'm trying to identify spectators that remain invisible.

I am washing Uri's wings and listening to the birdsong that comes from our human mouths, and I imagine then that this is all a rehearsal: a world in which I can press rewind and everything returns to some place before where it is now, and we—altogether, collectively, as one—together we live it again.

17

THE GHOST OF BIRDS: *[Indecipherable.]*

16

The triplets and I are at the star house. It's been busy this past week, townsfolk visiting each day. The line at noon, full of MAYBE people and their children, has each day snaked around the field, and to my surprise and pleasure, the people made sure the line runs by Saturn.

Today, though, there is no line, everyone out looking for Earth. I put the triplets inside, and when I try to get in with them, they won't let me. They want to be alone, they insist, and I slide the top over them and let them be there, be with the night sky in the middle of the day.

I sit on the ground, rest my back against the wall of the star house. In the distance, I can see the MAYBE people making their orbits.

My head is against the wall and I am listening to my handheld two-way radio. Then, quietly and subtly before it amplifies, I hear strange whispering. It is peculiar, the way the whispers unfold. It sounds something like a lilting conversation in a language I don't know and something like an a cappella song.

I try to follow the sound—I try to move my head to make it so that I can hear better—and then I stand up. I walk around a bit, until I have put my ear to the star house, because—am I surprised?—it is coming from inside.

I slide the lid off quickly and there the three of them are—lying down, their heads meeting in the center.

"Who were you talking to?" I ask them. "There is nobody here," I say and in saying, realize I have answered my own question.

"They were talking about you," One of the Triplets says.

"They were telling us what happens to you next," Another of the Triplets says.

"Who is they?" I ask the three beings who came from my body.

"They talk to us all the time," One of the Triplets says.

"You can hear them if you listen," Another of the Triplets says.

"Please answer my question."

And The Third of the Triplets says: "They are the ghost of birds."

15

Uri and I are on our front porch drinking a beer.

"Remember when you asked me why insurance?"

I nod my head.

"I told you I fell into it. Which is true. But also, it grew on me. Insurance," he says then, "is like this invisible protectant. You get to help people feel better about the future, let them make their mistakes and take the wrong path and let the world screw them and you get to help them find a way to recover. Puts a person's mind at ease, knowing they have a net to fall into, just in case," he says, and takes a swig of his beer. "An extremely expensive net."

And then Uri does something he doesn't do often, which is that he looks directly into my eyes, into my face, my flesh mask. Uri looks at me, and he is asking me to read him, and I can—I can see that he's recognized that this has to stop, that his identity as Icarus must be severed from his identity as the person with whom I share this duplex, with whom I am raising these triplets.

I see in his eyes this realization and then I say very quietly, "It might be time for curtain call."

He shakes his head. "Strike," he says.

"What's that?"

"The taking apart of the set after the run is over." Then he stands up and he starts to shake his shoulders a bit.

This is how Uri sheds his wings.

14

In the tower, at the window's ledge. Day.

> *ICARUS faces the audience, which is the window.*
> *His father is already gone, having just taken flight. He*
> *raises his wings. He makes a sound that could be a beat*
> *of laughter or could be a sob. On his face is a look that is*
> *impossible to decipher. It could be a smile or a frown. It*
> *could be both.*
>
> *He puts his wings down, and the sound of a bird can*
> *be heard. He raises them again, crouches as if to jump,*
> *and then he gasps—*

Curtain.

The End.

13

It is rare that I visit the nests alone, but it's just me inside the American robin's nest, legs pulled up to my chest. I am here, in this nest, the place a bird makes for their young, and I am thinking about this idea of home, what home means to me, what a home is. Is home the duplex, this town, the country, the world, our galaxy? Is home my flesh costume, the body I call my own?

If my body is a form of home, is the air I take into my lungs that lets me operate, is that air also, somehow, home? And the light I use to see the world around me, the sound that enters my head and in entering makes my brain compute that this or that is happening, this or that is getting closer or moving farther away. Maybe home is the space I am led to in my dreams, a structure my body creates without my permission.

It strikes me that there are all these dimensions of home, these concentric circles of home. It makes sense to care about all of those circles. It feels right to care about all these concentric circles, home both the elegant structure of my bones and also the solar system.

But some mornings, I find my head and heart don't have the capacity to care equally for them all. Sometimes I have to choose a circle. I need to focus on one in order to sustain myself so that later I can care about another.

The truth is I don't know if I am right. I'm not the one to give out advice—I'm the one who always needs it. But I also think this conundrum exists, this thinking always both about the body and the galaxy, the scope and the scale of The Crisis, the way we're at its tipping point.

The conundrum exists.

The conundrum being how to get out of bed each day knowing all the cruelty and horror of the world is unfolding around you, knowing humans are hurting humans in small and large ways in the house next door, the next town over, across the ocean on another continent.

The conundrum being bringing three new humans into the world knowing there are problems in this life that will still exist long after they are dead and gone, problems they cannot escape, that they may participate in—unconsciously—because the problems are bound to the way the world has been shaped.

The conundrum being that there are no longer birds, that the stars are no longer visible.

The conundrum being that I can't change the world.

I can't change the world, but I am in it.

And I guess in that regard, I already have.

12

Three knocks on the wall as I'm trying to wrangle the triplets to get downstairs.

When Uri comes over, it is without his wings, but he tells me the performance is still on. "Don't worry," he says, "I'm not starring in it." This evening's performance, he tells me, will be a bit delayed— the curtain opening at 8:20 p.m.

"Uri, that's late. Is anyone going to come?"

"People will come," he says. "I'm going to the community center to spread the word." He takes his wings with him, but he holds them in his hands. They are no longer part of his body.

He also takes a pile of small bits of recycled paper on which he has written the new time. I see him put one in each of our neighbors' mailboxes.

That evening, when we are in the folding chairs and lying on blankets in the field, I realize that to the left of the stage is Saturn and to the right is Sulien's star house, and behind us is the yellow warbler nest. This is how I come to know that I am surrounded by art. And while I know art won't fix anything, it has been my experience that it soothes the hurt.

Before we took our spaces in the field—before the rest of the town showed up—the triplets wanted to send Uri luck. He knelt down and hugged each one, and then all three of them pointed at something behind him and he looked at where their fingers ended. They shook their heads and started moving their fingers, and it took me a minute to realize that they were outlining the invisible wings on his back. They smiled and he mimed the heft of the wings and they laughed and then he stood up and shook the invisible wings off himself and pointed to them on the ground. Then he picked them up and handed them to the triplets and they stroked them slowly while he walked away.

Uri comes on stage—wingless—and we quiet down. Uri an-

nounces that tonight's performance is the first of a new kind of theater, his ultimate play with respect to The Crisis. He stands to the side
and tells us the performance will begin now, and he pulls the rope
that opens the curtains, and on the other side is the sun, just starting
to dip into the horizon. We clap and then we are silent, but nothing
is happening. Uri sits in a folding chair to stage right (which is really to his left, I realize then—life, I am coming to understand, is all
about how one chooses to see) and we wait and we wait and we watch
and we watch and the sun is going down bit by bit, dipping into the
horizon, and the colors start to look beautiful but we're uncomfortable because we do not do well with the ongoing delay. There is a
great deal of anticipation, of expectation. The silence grows longer
and longer then suddenly, like a flood of understanding, something
changes in the feeling of the audience. It's the first time I've really
noticed I'm part of an audience, that our bodies gathered together
constitute a different kind of being: a crowd, a collective, a flock. I
can feel it. It feels different than my body being alone. It's akin to the
feeling I used to get when the bus was full.

Then someone behind me yells a hoot and people start to clap
and I look at the stage to see if I've missed something. I look to see if
someone has entered the domain of mimesis, as Uri would say. But
I see nothing, just the sun. I nudge Luce and she says nothing but
when I look over she is smiling. I have not seen her smile that fully in
a long time. And she whispers, "Don't you get it?"

I do not get it. I am not getting it, even as I have listened to
Uri's theories of theater, which derive from the same etymology, I am
remembering now—*theory* and *theater*, "a way of seeing, or a lens"—
and then Luce helps me to see: "The sun," she says. "It's setting."

I breathe in deeply and shiver because yes, the sun is setting but
of course that's an illusion. It's the Earth that moves.

This is the performance, and we sit there and watch it and though
I don't see it at that time, though I don't know what is unfolding behind me and within the larger scope of the crowd, Uri tells me later

that he watched the MAYBE people wrap their arms around each other and he watched the children smile and point and he watched the elders among us, the very oldest, who have witnessed in our community and our region, in our world the very most change, he watched them let tears run down their cheeks. Others mouthed sentences that were for no one but them and many stood.

I stay seated, but I let myself forget myself as I watch the world around me do its work. We are watching a sunset through a human frame, I think, the theater curtains pulled back, and it is both an illusion and real. One of the Triplets cups their tiny hand to my ear and whispers, "The sky is falling," and I think, it is—the sky is falling, and there are no birds and there are no stars but there will always be this.

Uri isn't watching the sun. What he is watching is us. He's watching us watch the framed evening set in, and suddenly my head goes swimmy because I can't tell which of us is which—if we're watching the performance or he is.

Every person stays until the sky has turned a hue of bruise and then the sun is gone and the fireflies come out in the field and we clap. We clap and then Uri very slowly pulls the curtain closed and we all rise, and all of us—our whole town, together—all of us use the fireflies as light to navigate the way out of that field and back to the places we call home.

11

THE GHOST OF BIRDS: *[Indecipherable.]*

10

We are at the star house. The line of MAYBE people and their young is extraordinary. Sulien keeps a sand timer and walks up the ladder and lifts the kids in and out. Since Uri's last performance, the townsfolk have decided unanimously this is an experience the children should have alone, each child put inside by themselves to see the imaginary night sky. The children, to my surprise, are not scared. They do this and when they emerge, while they don't say much about their experience, something is different in the way they look at their parents. It is a kind of awe for what they must have witnessed when they themselves were children and it is a kind of sorrow that it was their generation and the ones before it that let the real night sky disappear.

When the triplets and I reach Sulien, he lifts them each in and closes the lid. Then he sets his sand timer, which counts just five minutes. He flips it twice, for a total of ten minutes for each star house show.

"Great turnout today," I tell him.

"You notice the way the kids look at their parents?" and I tell him that I do. "Wonder what they'd think if they knew about my generation," he says then, and I ask him what he means.

"When Luce and your dad and I were young, we could see more than just the stars. Back then, from this town, you could see the whole galaxy. The Milky Way, the colors of all that light, the clumps of stars so dense they lit up the night world. That band of stars running through the center of the sky like a ring of speckled light. The Milky Way was so vibrant throughout this town it never actually got dark."

I had never known this about my town. Of course, I had assumed that once, long ago, the Milky Way was visible, but never did I imagine it could be seen within the lifetime of my father and Sulien and Luce.

"Things change quickly," he says, watching the sand move in the timer.

"Sure do," I say, and I adjust the handheld two-way radio in the front pocket of my overalls. "The hourglass is a strange contraption."

Sulien nods his head. "One of the oldest ways humans have kept time. That and the sundial. What's interesting to me," Sulien says, watching the sand move from the top to the bottom, "is the way that you turn it 180 degrees. You have to do it twice to make the sand return to its origins, to make it go the full 360."

I think then of the sign in my grandfathers' workshop, the workshop that now belongs to Luce. "180 degrees," I say, "is a half-circle. But also, it's essentially a line."

Sulien nods.

And then, he says it. He says what I have been waiting for him to say for months now. He opens the door that has only been cracked between us. He pulls the door open wide.

"My partner—" he says and he takes a deep breath in and then a deep breath out. His eyes get red around the rims. "My partner—you remember her?" I nod very slowly that I do. "She used to love them. Hourglasses. Had them all over the house. A useful reminder, she'd say, that the minute we are born the clock is on and it's all just a ticking down from there."

I want to say something about his partner and my father, but I don't because I realize I don't have to. Not right now. Sulien has opened the door and it is for him to decide if I should enter his space or he should enter mine and how we'll manage to share our past pain gently, so that it becomes something we invite each other to know rather than keep locked up.

For now, we are watching a device measure the passage of time as the sand dissolves on the top and the sand collects on the bottom and then, just like that, the sand's slow and steady travel comes to an abrupt end.

"The turning point," Sulien says. He looks at me for a really long time—he looks at me with a face that feels like a promise—and then he flips the timer over, and starts it all over again.

9

There is a very complex version of Girl in Glass Vessel that I read a long time ago. It is so different from the old folktale, it was difficult at first to discern that the version was actually a retelling of the story at all.

I remember being deeply moved by it, and finding it both surreal and haunting. But I do not remember any of the details—merely that I had read the book just once and it was only many years later, many, many years later, that I realized what it was retelling.

The Only Person I've Ever Loved was the one who told me.

I'd been describing the faint echo of the book as it resonated in my head. At first I couldn't even remember if I'd actually read it—it was like the trace of an echo of a memory, perhaps even less than that. I described the thin scaffolding of the story, and then suddenly she grabbed my arm.

"Of course! Yes, that book. Isn't that a Girl in Glass Vessel story?"

"No. I don't think so. I'm not sure. Is it?"

"Definitely."

"I— I hadn't realized," I told her, a bit shaken.

"But it's obvious. It's got all the major elements: the dead birds, the fake sky, a transparent container in which a girl is trapped."

"Yeah, but it's all hidden. It's all metaphorical. Also, I thought a major part of the girl in the transparent container was that she didn't know."

"Oh, no," said The Only Person I've Ever Loved, "that's what makes it tragic. That she knows." She started biting her nails, and I pulled her hand away from her mouth. "I mean, all the people around the girl know she's in the vessel. They are constantly gesturing toward it, constantly telling her they feel sorry for her for being in her vessel. You know?" But I didn't know. I hadn't understood the story that way at all. "I mean, if she didn't know, it wouldn't be tragedy."

"What would it be then?"

"Horror," she said.

"But at the end of this book I'm talking about, she doesn't get out of the container. She doesn't dissolve."

"No, no, no—you're reading the original all wrong. She never actually escapes the transparent vessel," said The Only Person I've Ever Loved.

"Of course she does! She dissolves from the rain or snow or tears of the planetarium—whichever version you're reading—and she becomes nothing."

"But the looping," said The Only Person I've Ever Loved. "Don't you get it? The story itself—the story is the transparent container. If you read the story as also a container, then the looping of the story—on repeat, told over and over again—that, too, is a kind of transparent orb. The real and true vessel in which she stays trapped."

I remember that evening I found myself walking through a kind of fog. This book, and the conversation it incited, this book I'd read so long ago that I'd only remembered the vaguest elements of—that story now seen through this new lens, changed everything.

It was not as though the folktale being transposed over the book had changed my reading.

It was as if the book had somehow changed the folktale retrospectively.

8

HER TWO-WAY RADIO: *[Static.]*

7

The theory of the Big Bang says that nothing in the world existed before this single moment in the long past when the universe burst into existence. But as all physicists know, the problem with the Big Bang is that it is an effect without a cause, which defies logic. Why did it start? What made it begin? What happened just before in order to create it, and thus create us?

There is, of course, an answer to this question, but we don't know it. All we know is that this moment marked the beginning of entropy, and ever since then, order has been moving toward chaos, structures have been moving toward rubble, harmony has been moving toward dissonance.

There is one theory that the Big Bang isn't actually The Beautiful Beginning, that it was just one blip in an endless cycle of openings and closings, expansions and contractions. The theory says, essentially, that time is not straight.

But no one believes that physicist and the theory is considered a fiction.

6

"Why do you think," The Only Person I've Ever Loved once asked me, "your déjà vu is so bad?"

She asked me this often, but I'd never really thought about it until this moment. She was always wanting to know when it happened. Is it happening now? she'd ask. Now? Sometimes I would tell her when it did, but sometimes I wouldn't. I felt like I had so little for myself then, and I wanted some of these experiences to be mine alone.

This day, we weren't in the yard of my grandfathers, that galaxy of earths, but at the local library, where we would spend many days during the summer because of the free air conditioning. We would lounge in the children's section, lying on our backs, puffing our candy cigarettes—the fine dust from the white powdered candy stick looking like genuine smoke—until a child would tell us there's no smoking in the building and that would be our signal to eat the white sticks and the child would make big eyes or seem grossed out or run away and we would pull another one out of the package.

"Why do you think your déjà vu is so bad?" she asked me, and I'd responded that I didn't know.

But lately I've wondered if perhaps I do know, did know, knew even then. It's part of this alignment I've been feeling, this notion that things are coming into a kind of order that has been en route since the eclipse and maybe even before then. Maybe the entirety of this life of mine, this life that I believe myself to be living.

The night The Only Person I've Ever Loved asked me this—I must have been eleven or twelve, it was after my father was gone—that night in bed I had a really long episode. By which I mean it wasn't just a thirty-second sensation, but a sequence of events, events I was sure I had lived before, though they also felt new. I wrote some sentences on a piece of paper and it felt both new and redundant. I stood up and went to the window, hummed a tune, took a sweater out of the closet and put it on, then took it off, pulled a book from the shelf, tried to surprise myself with whatever it was that I would do next, but all of it—all of it felt both new and redundant. It was the longest episode of déjà vu I'd had until that point, and it had lasted almost an hour.

Ever since the eclipse, my déjà vu comes in long blocks of time. A whole meal, a long afternoon, the duration of one of my last shifts driving Route 0.

Last week, it was a full day. A full day that was both my first time meeting it and also aged, familiar, recognizable. Already known.

The sound of space is filling up the room of the triplets and my handheld two-way radio has been on for weeks now, sitting in the front pocket of my overalls, close to my heart. I am in the triplets' rocker, moving back and forth, and I am listening to space—the whooshing and groaning of space, which I realize then is probably the exact sound unfolding inside of my body, inside my veins.

I rock in my chair and I turn my head to look toward my window where the globe Luce made me lives next to my telescope. Pangea.

And then I think of Maxwell–Heaviside equations and Thomson scattering. The sound of weeping icebergs.

Electromagnetism and fluid dynamics. The smell of cigarette smoke.

Quarks and leptons and the Boltzmann constant. The taste of cinnamon nutmeg chocolate chip cookies.

The stretchmarks on my stomach when I was pregnant. The patterns of the worry lines on my father's face. Sitting in the driver's seat of the bus for the last time.

Sitting in the driver's seat of the bus for the first time.

Never is not the opposite of now. The opposite of never is always, I think, and spin Pangea gently with my hand.

5

THE ONLY PERSON SHE'S EVER LOVED: *[Stage right, seated on a plane, heading toward whatever city she calls home. Her text to Sulien can be seen by the audience via a digital screen above the stage.]* She's the only person I've ever loved and I never told her.

SULIEN: *[Stage left, tending to one of the nests. The sound of a ping to indicate an incoming message. He pulls his phone from his pocket, reads, looks up at the sky. He types back a response that is displayed above him for the audience to see.]* You may be right about the first part, but you're wrong about the second.

4

I can't know the future, but I know enough about the past to understand one causes the other. Sometimes I wish I could stay always where I am right now, in an eternal present.

Earth remains missing. We are starting to get the feeling it always will be, and the formal orbits around the community have only increased in frequency. All of our eyes are to the ground. We may find it one day, or it might never be revealed at all. As long as the possibility of Earth looms on the horizon, the town remains full of MAYBE.

When the triplets ask me why everyone is so busy looking at the ground, I tell them it's because they're looking for Earth and Uri tries to explain to them that this is called irony and Luce tells them to help her pick up all this litter because nature's not going to heal from humans by itself and Sulien gives me a look that tells me he believes it will.

We spend every Saturday evening watching the earth spin until the sun becomes invisible beneath the horizon. These days it feels disquieting, but the sun as a rule is disquieting, so we all work hard to see it through a lens that is both troubled and full of awe.

Tonight, after the sun fell from the sky, after the sun nested into the invisible world below the horizon, the triplets looked at me and I wondered a very strange thing. I wondered if in fact The Crisis is over, has been for a while. What if this is no longer The Crisis, I thought, and The Catastrophe is already here.

As we walk home, making a loop for good luck around the sundial in the center of town, I consider that in the whole of my life, all my years on Earth, Saturn has not once made a single, complete orbit around the sun. One year on Saturn takes twenty-nine years here and one day I will be twenty-nine and Saturn will be sitting on the plane of the Milky Way in precisely the same spot as the day I was born. Will it have changed at all in twenty-nine years?

But then, I think, taking another loop around the sundial for extra good luck: girl, bad, curse, bird. There is no time on Saturn. Time is a human invention.

3

Of all the endings Uri wrote for his play, there is one that feels most true.

I found it one day when I was picking up after the triplets, the manuscript having slipped to the floor. There in the mess of pages was a single page with all the text crossed out, an X through the whole thing. And I did something I shouldn't have. I read it.

The ending is this: Icarus plunges into the ocean. He thinks the water feels like sand against his body, and he imagines he is moving through the thinnest part of an hourglass, from the top of the glass to the bottom. It is only then—in the final moment of his life—that he realizes the strange logic of an hourglass: that if the sand is time, it moves from the future on the top to the past.

It lets me imagine that maybe, somewhere out there, history is moving conversely, and soon, very soon, the universe will give birth to a new species that instills in us the longing to fly while reminding us that we never will.

2

THE GHOST OF BIRDS: *[Indecipherable. Or is it?]*

1

The last step in making a globe is adding the equator. It is a thin band that runs through the thickest part of our sphere, imaginary but present in the human mind, just like all the borders of the countries, all the imaginary designations between where things begin and end. The globe is primarily a fiction, but it's also a reminder of how we might get some perspective, get beyond our smallness to see a grander picture, to recognize how arbitrary these artificial limits are. The equator is added to cover the seam between the hemispheres, to hide the fact that this miniature earth is a construction.

This is what I'm thinking when I reach Saturn. It is the dead of night and though I cannot see the stars, I know they're up there, just like the real ringed orb of Saturn. Saturn is just over one light hour away and so I decide to sit on the grass and wait for the light to travel. The light from Saturn would travel for all this time, this full hour, to reach me here on Earth.

I have my handheld two-way radio close—I have kept it on, and I've been listening—and I sit near Saturn and wait. I wait for someone's frequency to meet mine and for our connections to align. Perhaps I will connect with someone in this town or the next one over, the next region or country, another hemisphere. Or perhaps I will connect with someone outside of all this, someone larger and more powerful than myself.

I wait and the light seconds are passing, the light minutes are passing, and the light hour is just about up, and I start to hear something. The static shifts a bit, then seems to go away. I put my ear to the pores of the radio and turn up the volume. My body is throbbing with anticipation and dread.

I hear something then, and what I hear is surreal. It is a human—sure as rain—it is a human breathing.

Uri has told me about how the actor knows what is going to happen next, has rehearsed this for months, but the character—the person the actor is playing—they don't know what is coming. They have no knowledge of what is going to unfold next, and part of the work of acting is trying to eliminate the actor-identity and give yourself over completely to the character-identity, so that you forget you know what is going to happen, which way your body is going to go on the stage, what words you're about to say. You have to abandon the you that is actor, give yourself over to the you that is character. That, Uri says, is when the enchantment supersedes the illusion and something clicks for the person in the audience and the character in the story and the actor on the stage.

That is what I'm thinking when I look up. I am thinking I don't know what is going to happen next.

I am in the field and I am looking up and listening and my blood. How it aches. My veins are aching, and the ache is real.

It feels like I am standing on top of the earth, which I am, always have been, but it feels different now.

And then—

The trees begin to stretch.

They stretch impossibly until they are great streaks of bark and leaf. Time is slowing but also the world is extending itself, stretching like taffy or smearing like paint. The field expands and the limit between the sky and land becomes incalculable, and everything elongates and doubles, triples its length. I want to be unsettled, but my déjà vu tells me this is all as it was meant to be. My body stretches and my mind stretches and what I feel and see is everything all at once.

I am alone in a field and I am coming to understand that I am alone in several ways. I am me and this is it and yet—despite everything stretching and smearing, extending and reaching, even my body—despite the way I expand and become so much larger, I see something out there that is not stretched like elastic or glass in its liquid state. Something is defying the logic of the way time and space are folded into one another.

What I see before me—what I behold—is everything, even me, moving in reverse.

First it is the MAYBE people orbiting the town over and over, walking backward. Then the cleft in the board at the community center grows larger and larger until there are two sides. Sulien un-paints the walls of the star house, erases the holes until he walks backward from the field to town, replaces the wood on the shelves of the hardware store. The sun rises at night, rises at night, over and over and we watch it, then walk backward to our homes. The previous Saturday, Uri is on stage, sweating and stammering through Icarus's lines and The Demonstration has a small group on either side, then a crowd the previous Saturday, then all of the town's young adult people the Saturday before that.

The Only Person I've Ever Loved steps off my bus, then onto it. I drive the bus over and over in reverse, led by the bumper, the front trailing behind.

The nests start to go missing. There are 14, then 10, then 3. I reach down to touch Saturn and then I go out to the field over and over again, never move beyond the dead end of the road.

One morning there are no nests and the bus begins to fill with people and the duplex becomes emptied of our things. I hug Uri hello, and then we walk away from each other very slowly, in reverse, the smiles fading from our faces.

The eclipse comes and then everyone anticipates its coming. The Demonstration swells with people each weekend, nothing getting resolved.

The triplets grow smaller and smaller, tiny, and move back inside me. And then there are their parents, alive and loving each other, and me pulling pieces of cake from my mouth with a fork and placing them in perfect triangles onto a plate.

In the sky, a bird. Then several birds flocking together, and then not—then birds flying separately, hundreds moving about in the world above.

The Only Person I've Ever Loved is writing on my back with her finger and the tears move from my wet shirt to my cheeks, then get vacuumed up into my eyes.

And my father is alive in bed struggling, and then he is out of bed working his shifts at The Factory, and then he is reading me novels, the pages flipping from left to right.

And then I am not born, and someone is planting the solar system inside our town. And then there is no town at all, and all the horror and roses and held hands and bowls of warm oatmeal and lips pressed against each other and sweaters and rocking chairs and ice cream sandwiches, all the guns and sorrow and blankets and looking into each other's eyes, all of it is moving in reverse, becoming undone.

I start to weep because, my god, the fact of being alive, the act of listening, of coming to understand, the act of making believe—

Then, suddenly—I am breathing and listening and I am seeing the sky—suddenly there is light. The night sky has split open, and what is beyond the cloudy cover is revealed. It has been an hour. The glass on top is empty of the sand. The sand that is the future is gone and my light hour is up.

There above me is the stars. But it is more than the stars—what I come to see is the whole of the universe, the Milky Way and everything it contains, its facts and its fictions. It is like some artificial covering has been removed and the whole of the sky in its rawness, in its realness, is revealed. I look up and I am watching everything elongate and collapse into its own center. I can't tell if the world is breaking apart and dissolving or if it's just now coming into the clearest kind of focus it ever has, and all this time, though I had my two-way radio, I wasn't really listening.

I see it now, I see everything, and I hear it and it is closing in. I see the center and the way the light that is the world bends and is consumed by that point, spirals around it. I think: this is it. This must be The Beautiful Beginning.

What I want to do is read that book, that complex, coded ver-

sion of Girl in Glass Vessel. I want that story to take me into whatever comes before.

My déjà vu is overwhelming, it is making me tilt like the earth,
and then, just like that, something gets flipped and I remember that
Luce once told me the etymology of her name meant *light* and also
Uri's and Sulien's, too, and it only strikes me now as strange, and
180 degrees is half of a circle but also a line and everything's a castle
in the air and then, through the radio in my hand comes a familiar
voice reading the first line of that old archaic story, then I hear that
story begin—

180

Luce once explained that her fathers taught her to compose a globe
like this:

ACKNOWLEDGMENTS

Thank you, Lauren Berlant for your 2011 work of cultural criticism *Cruel Optimism*. The concept of cruel optimism, as well as discussions of crisis, impasse, precarity, futurity, and the "perpetual present" gave language (and thus shape) to lived experiences I was trying to process and complicate in the writing of this book. For your work, I am grateful.

Thank you, Tower View Alternative High School in Red Wing Minnesota. Thanks in particular to the class of 1999 for making the solar system sculpture project. Thank you, Anderson Center at Tower View for letting me write and think and be. Thank you for putting up with me as I sought out—and in the very last hours of my residency, finally found—Earth.

Thank you to *The Iowa Review* and *The Threepenny Review* for first publishing small portions of this novel.

Thank you to the Bard Fiction Prize committee—Mary Copenegro, Bradford Morrow, and Benjamin Hale—for seeing something in my last book and letting me live in the woods for three months next to the John Cage archives in order to finish writing this one.

Thank you always and in an ongoing way to my students at the College of Charleston, the University of Utah, and UPEP (the University of Utah Prison Education Project).

Thank you, Emily Forland. I am hoping the next project won't be so weird.

Thank you, University of Utah Faculty Fellowship, for giving me time to dig into this strange project. Thank you to my colleagues in the English department.

Thank you, National Endowment for the Arts, for supporting this project with a fellowship. I am honored. I am grateful. You are wonderful.

Thank you, Ron Drager.

Thank you, Valerie Lindquist Drager.

Thank you, Leland Drager.

Thank you, Allan G. Borst.

Thank you, Michelle Dotter. For everything. Always and exponentially.

And finally, thank YOU. You, I mean. For reading this. You are appreciated. A book is a strange technology—one makes this object with a host of others, then hands it off and never really knows if it means something to someone someday. If you have read this far, then perhaps it has made its way, somehow, inside your mind or heart (which is the world). Thank you for being a reader. Thank you for reading books. I and a whole host of others—there are a lot of us out there!—very much appreciate you.

ABOUT THE AUTHOR

Lindsey Drager is the author of the novels *The Sorrow Proper* (Dzanc, 2015), *The Lost Daughter Collective* (Dzanc, 2017), and *The Archive of Alternate Endings* (Dzanc, 2019). Her books have been listed as a "Best Book of the Year" in *The Guardian* and NPR; twice been named finalists for Lambda Literary Awards; and have been translated into Spanish and Italian. Recipient of a 2017 Shirley Jackson Award, a 2020 National Endowment for the Arts Fellowship in Prose, and the 2022 Bard Fiction Prize, she is an assistant professor of creative writing at the University of Utah.